EXTRA
TIME

MORRIS GLEITZMAN

PUFFIN

PUFFIN BOOKS

Published by the Penguin Group
Penguin Books Ltd, 80 Strand, London WC2R 0RL, England
Penguin Group (USA) LLC, 375 Hudson Street, New York, New York 10014, USA
Penguin Group (Canada), 90 Eglinton Avenue East, Suite 700, Toronto, Ontario, Canada M4P 2Y3
(a division of Pearson Penguin Canada Inc.)
Penguin Ireland, 25 St Stephen's Green, Dublin 2, Ireland (a division of Penguin Books Ltd)
Penguin Group (Australia), 707 Collins Street, Melbourne, Victoria 3008, Australia
(a division of Pearson Australia Group Pty Ltd)
Penguin Books India Pvt Ltd, 11 Community Centre, Panchsheel Park, New Delhi – 110 017, India
Penguin Group (NZ), 67 Apollo Drive, Rosedale, Auckland 0632, New Zealand
(a division of Pearson New Zealand Ltd)
Penguin Books (South Africa) (Pty) Ltd, Block D, Rosebank Office Park, 181 Jan Smuts Avenue,
Parktown North, Gauteng 2193, South Africa

Penguin Books Ltd, Registered Offices: 80 Strand, London WC2R 0RL, England

pufinbooks.com

First published by Penguin Group (Australia) 2013
Published in Great Britain by Penguin Books 2014
002

Text copyright © Morris Gleitzman, 2013
Background cover illustrations copyright © PILart/Shutterstock.com and © Seyyahil/ Shutterstock.
com
Cartoon cover illustrations copyright © Dean Rankin, 2013
All rights reserved

The moral right of the author has been asserted

Cover and text design by Tony Palmer
Cover and text design copyright © Penguin Group (Australia)

Typeset in 13pt Minion
Printed in Great Britain by Clays Ltd, St Ives plc

British Library Cataloguing in Publication Data
A CIP catalogue record for this book is available from the British Library

ISBN: 978-0-141-35298-5

www.greenpenguin.co.uk

MIX
Paper from
responsible sources
FSC
www.fsc.org   FSC™ C018179

Penguin Books is committed to a sustainable
future for our business, our readers and our
planet. This book is made from paper certified
by the Forest Stewardship Council.

For Jono

Warm-Up

1

'Hey, Sutherland,' yells an unfriendly voice. 'If you got any last wishes, make 'em now.'

Matt and the others stop playing.

We all turn.

This waste ground next to the cattle yard is the best place in Australia for a kick-around. But it does get a bit crowded sometimes.

Coming towards us across the crunchy brown grass, dust puffing up from their boots, are six kids.

Big ones.

They're all wearing orange soccer shirts.

I sigh. Why can't people leave Matt alone? Sometimes I think he won't get any peace till every soccer show-off in town has tried to prove they're better than him.

'Your day of wrecking has arrived,' says the captain of the orange team to Matt.

'I think you mean day of reckoning,' says Matt.

'Get your words right,' I say to the orange captain.

The orange captain ignores me. That happens quite a bit when you're a younger sister.

The orange kids are all glaring at Matt as if they don't like him, which is really unfair. They don't even know him.

'Come on,' sneers the captain to Matt. 'Let's see how good you really are. Your lot against us.'

I wait for Matt to tell them to get lost. But he doesn't. He's extremely good-natured. Which is pretty amazing given what he's been through.

I'm not so good-natured.

'Get lost,' I say to the orange lot. 'We're in the middle of a game if you haven't noticed.'

'We're not here to get lost,' smiles the orange captain. 'We're here to shred your butts.'

I'm always amazed by our town. It's not very big, but the people are so different from each other. Some of them are really nice, but some of them, like this orange lot, look like they've never had a cuddle in their lives.

Mum and Dad reckon it's because so many families tragically break up.

Uncle Cliff says there's another reason. Too many big dogs in this town. Too many people have them in their houses as pets, he reckons, and they have to fight with them to get any food.

'Excuse me,' I say to the orange captain. 'We're not doing butt-shredding. We're just playing for fun.'

'See, I told you,' says the captain to his team-mates.

'Matt Sutherland is just a cluck cluck red rooster chicken coward.'

'With a haggle for a kid sister,' says another one.

'The word's haggis,' I say. 'If you mean the Scottish sausage made from sheep's guts.'

The orange kids all snigger.

I try to ignore them. I know what they're laughing at. My tartan skirt. Mum got it for me from the charity shop because two of my grandparents were Scottish before they got old and died. In my family we like to remember people who aren't with us any more.

Matt is giving the orange team a thoughtful look.

I think a couple of them actually have got dog bites on their faces. Either that or they've been practising shaving with gardening equipment.

The rest of our lot are giving the orange team a look too. It's not a look they usually give people. I think they want to take up the challenge.

I grab Matt's arm and pull him over to where the others can't hear us.

What I should say to him is, 'Matt, it's too dangerous, they're as big as double fridges and there's no ref and you've got metal pins in your legs.' Which is true, and it's what Mum would want me to say.

But Matt would hate it if I said that. He doesn't like anyone making a big deal about his car crash injuries. He doesn't mind people looking at the scars on his legs, but not if they get all concerned.

So instead I just say, 'Come on, the sun's getting too hot, let's go and visit Uncle Cliff.'

Matt shakes his head.

'People who run away,' he says, 'next thing they know, they're living under their bed.'

Matt's fourteen, so he says stuff like that.

I sigh again and take the sunblock out of my skirt pocket and hand it to him. Part of me admires Matt for giving it a go. Part of me wishes he was safely under a bed right now.

We walk back to the orange bruisers.

I just hope if it gets rough, Matt's skill will keep him out of danger.

We've had too much tragedy in our family already.

We don't want any more.

2

While Matt and the others decide who'll be in our team, I quickly think of a game plan. The orange kids are very big. And they look like the sort of kids who don't get the difference between a soccer tackle (going for the ball with their foot) and a rugby tackle (going for your body parts with their body parts).

'Fast passing,' I whisper to Matt. I also whisper it to Jayden and Zac and Celine and Callum and Gael-Anne.

They all give me a nod.

'Haggis not playing with us?' says one of the dog's breakfasts, looking at me.

'Bridie gets asthma,' says Matt.

Which is true, he's not just saying that. If I run, I turn into a medical emergency, so I've promised Mum I won't.

The orange team kick off.

They do some passes, but not very good ones. They've all got muscles, but not much balance. Dad's an expert furniture removal man and he can tell with one glance if an item is top-heavy and wobbly. If he was moving this lot he'd definitely strap them down in the truck.

The orange kids do another pass and Matt nips between them and gets the ball. One of them tries to kick it away from him. Matt does what he usually does when somebody tries to tackle him. Sways his hips and glides past like an expert removal man getting a big wardrobe through a small door.

'Stop him,' yells the grumpy orange captain.

But Matt is halfway down the pitch. He does a short pass to Jayden, who isn't having a good week. Jayden's mum is in hospital. Jayden passes back to Matt. Matt whisks the ball past two defenders and passes to Jayden again because regular touches of the ball help take your mind off things when your mum's having an operation.

Jayden could go for goal but he obviously doesn't feel up to it, so he passes back to Matt.

Matt could score with his eyes closed and one foot in his back pocket, but he doesn't either. He dribbles across the front of the goal, past lots of orange tackles, doing lots of skill to control the ball because wombats have been at the pitch, and gently taps it to Gael-Anne, who isn't having a good week either because her family's washing got stolen, including her sports bra.

6

Gael-Anne kicks, misses the ball, kicks again, and scores.

Her grin is so big we all have to grin too.

The orange kids aren't grinning.

I think they're a bit stunned. People get like that when they see Matt play.

'Dumbos,' their captain yells at them. 'How many times do I have to tell you? Go in hard.'

The orange team are looking hot and miserable. We're all hot because it's nearly ten in the morning, but it's probably worse when you've got a grumpy captain.

I go over to him.

'Excuse me,' I say. 'We don't do rough tackles.'

The grumpy captain squints at me.

'Who are you?' he says. 'The referee?'

I shake my head. That's dopey. You don't need a referee when you're playing for fun.

'She's our manager,' says Matt.

I've never thought of it like that. But it's sort of true. I keep an eye on Matt for Mum and Dad and give the players advice and sometimes I get everyone water from the drinking fountain.

'Time to swap sides,' I say to Matt.

The orange team look confused, but Matt knows what I'm talking about.

'OK,' he says. He turns to the biggest orange boy. 'You and me swap?'

'Hang about,' says the grumpy orange captain. 'What's going on? You can't change sides once a match has officially started.'

'This isn't a match,' I say. 'It's a game.'

'We always do it,' says Matt. 'When my side scores, I swap over to make it fairer.'

'So it's a better game,' says Gael-Anne. 'Not so one-sided.'

'More fun,' I explain.

'No way,' says the grumpy captain.

Me and Matt and our lot look at each other and shrug. We don't get it. What's the point of soccer if you're not enjoying it?

The orange team kick off again.

'Jeez,' says a voice behind me. 'They're big.'

It's Uncle Cliff. He usually keeps an eye on us while we're playing. His house overlooks the showground, and since he lost his job and Aunty Paula left him, he spends a lot of time on his verandah.

'It's OK,' I say. 'We're doing fast passing.'

Uncle Cliff knows a lot about sport. He watches about a thousand hours of it a week on TV.

The orange team have got the ball, and their biggest player is powering towards Matt with it.

'Come on, Sutherland,' says the big orange kid. 'Tackle me.'

Matt just backs off, keeping his eye on the ball.

Uncle Cliff is feeling tense, I can tell. He's holding his beer can so tight it's crinkling.

'Don't worry,' I say. 'Matt's too skilful. They can't touch him even when they go for him.'

I know Matt won't go for the big orange kid. Matt has promised Mum no rough tackles and he always keeps a promise.

'Take it off me,' says the big orange kid to Matt.

Matt still holds back.

They're close to the goal now.

Suddenly the big orange kid shoots. Matt blocks the shot. The ball spins towards Celine in goal. She catches it, then another orange kid barges into her and sends her sprawling. Luckily she falls onto one of her goal posts, which is a pile of Zac's mum's washing from the laundromat.

The ball bounces out of her arms.

Matt pounces on it, whisks it past a couple of orange players, and shoots from very long range.

Up the other end the orange goalie blinks. That's all he has time to do as the ball flashes past him.

'Rock 'n' roll,' says Uncle Cliff. 'Good goal.'

The orange kids are just staring. They've probably never seen anyone score from the middle of the pitch before.

'Are you OK, Celine?' I say, hurrying over to where Matt's helping her up.

She nods, rubbing her leg.

'OK, Damian,' says Uncle Cliff, going over to the orange kid who flattened Celine. 'Here's your choice. If you want violence you can go and rent one of those video games where you play soccer and kill aliens at the same time, or you can stay here and play decent. Up to you.'

9

'Sorry, Cliff,' mumbles the orange kid.

Uncle Cliff used to work at the electrical store before it closed, so he knows most people in town. And everyone knows him because of his Rolling Stones hair, which is inspired by a very old rock group Uncle Cliff likes. It's a sort of tufty hairstyle with bits of jewellery and little feathers tied to the ends of some of the tufts.

The orange team are looking really miserable. They've done what they came to do, see how good Matt really is, and now they're probably wondering what it's going to feel like to lose twenty–nil.

None of us want that.

I make a manager decision.

'It's getting a bit hot for running around,' I say. 'Let's play blindfold penalties.'

Our lot all like the idea.

I explain to the orange team about blindfold penalties. How the kicker and the goalie both wear blindfolds, so it's a very entertaining type of penalty.

Their captain looks doubtful, but the rest of his team look relieved.

Everyone enjoys themselves heaps. Even the grumpy captain. By the time he's taken a few penalties he isn't even grumpy any more. He doesn't even care when he slices a kick so high it goes over the fence into the cattle yard next door.

'Good Aussie Rules kick,' says Matt. 'Don't worry, I'll get it.'

Matt heads off towards the fence.

'Matt,' I yell.

Uncle Cliff yells at him too.

Members of the public aren't allowed in the cattle yard, specially not kids.

'Matt,' I yell again.

But it's too late. He's already over the fence.

I'm getting a sick feeling in my guts.

Most managers get it sometimes. It's the fear of losing. With me it's a bit different.

I don't mind losing a football match.

There's something much more important I don't want to lose.

3

M e and Uncle Cliff sprint to the fence.
'Don't run,' says Uncle Cliff to me. 'You'll stress your pipes.'

I can feel asthma coming on, but I have to risk it. Matt is already in the cattle yard.

I can't see any cattle, which is good. But I can see people, which isn't good. If they spot Matt, he's in big trouble.

Next to the office, standing in the back of a truck, is a bloke with a microphone. His voice starts echoing out from the auctioneer's loudspeaker. A crowd of people are listening to him, a couple with cameras.

'Some politician up from the city,' says Uncle Cliff as we climb over the cattle yard fence. 'Probably here to tell us the Chinese have bought another million tonnes of our beef.'

Now I'm nearer, I can see our ball sitting right in the middle of one of the big empty cattle pens.

There's Matt, climbing over the chutes towards it. Just as he reaches it, I hear something else.

Grumpy bellowing. Even louder than the orange team in a bad mood.

'Oh Jeez,' mutters Uncle Cliff.

I see where the bellowing is coming from.

Crashing along one of the chutes, stampeding out into the pen towards Matt, are a mob of cattle, huge ones. A million tonnes of beef at least. The cattle look like they're in a panic. They probably think they're on their way to the abattoir to be turned into rissoles and wallets.

Matt sees the cattle and freezes. He looks like a skinny rabbit on a highway, blinking at trucks thundering down on him, trucks with horns and snot.

'Matt,' I scream.

We run towards the pen. I'm starting to struggle for breath. Sometimes there's not much difference between asthma and terror.

Some of the crowd are screaming at Matt too.

I try to think of a game plan for him.

Run for it, Matt.

Too late, the cattle are too close.

Lie on the ground, Matt. Curl up and put your arms over your head.

No good, you'll be trampled.

'Matt,' I yell again.

Matt doesn't do either of my game plans. He does his own.

As the cattle surge around him, snorting and swiping at him with their horns, Matt starts moving the ball from foot to foot, swaying his hips, tilting his shoulders, crouching, turning, keeping his balance, using his arms as well as his feet, dodging the horns and the huge crushing bodies, gliding the ball through the bellowing herd, doing more skill than I've ever seen him do, and that's saying a lot.

A huge lot.

Everyone is frozen now, just watching him.

I start to breathe again.

Matt flicks the ball high into the air, ducks between a couple of metal bars, and waits outside the pen to gracefully catch the ball on his knee, which he does.

Most of the people applaud. A couple of officials glare at him angrily.

I rush over and throw my arms round him.

'Don't ever do that again,' I say.

Matt is sweaty, but grinning.

'Don't tell Mum,' he says.

He knows I won't. He knows I wouldn't dream of it. Not even next time I get cross with him for making the toilet roll soggy playing soccer with it in the bathroom.

Uncle Cliff arrives.

'Matty,' he says. 'Are you alright?'

Matt nods, still grinning.

The angry officials start to have a go at Uncle

Cliff, probably because they think he's Matt's parent or guardian. Uncle Cliff steers them away from us.

Matt's grin disappears. I know why. He's worried they'll tell Mum and Dad.

'It's OK,' I say. 'Uncle Cliff's calming them down.'

We watch Uncle Cliff calming down the angry officials.

'Fair go,' Uncle Cliff is saying to them. 'If you want cattle running round for the news cameras, you should have warning signs. Health and safety, page one. And production assistants with luminous vests.'

Uncle Cliff is good with angry people. He reckons it's a skill you develop in electrical stores because of the damage electricity does to some electrical products.

Matt is rubbing himself on the shoulder. He sees me notice.

'One of the cattle pronged me,' he says.

I check him out. But there's no blood. His shirt isn't even torn. Which is a huge relief.

'Doesn't hurt much,' says Matt. 'No need to panic.'

Sometimes older brothers can be really dumb. Matt should know by now why I panic. He's had nearly two and a half years to work it out.

It's because I'm scared of losing him as well.

4

After Mum and Dad finish work, we tidy Pete and Danny's graves like we do every Sunday afternoon.

Dad sweeps, Mum does the flowers, Matt pulls out the weeds and I pick the tree seeds out of the gravel. Birds poo the seeds out. They don't do it on purpose. It's something they were born with, like Matt scoring goals.

Mum hates having any sort of tree seeds on the graves. I think it's because it was a tree that killed Pete and Danny. That and an out-of-control cattle truck with brake pads Uncle Cliff reckons probably came from a pizza shop.

Today Matt is quiet as he weeds.

I know why. His shoulder must be getting stiff, which happens when you've nearly been killed by cattle, and he doesn't want Mum to see.

I try to cheer things up a bit.

'Dad,' I say, 'tell us a Pete and Danny story.'

On Sunday afternoons Mum and Dad often tell us things about when Pete and Danny were little. The twins were eleven years older than me and I wasn't born when they were small, so it's a way for me and Matt to get to know them better.

Dad smiles and wipes the sweat off his face with his hand. I love the way his hands are so big. He'd have made a great goalkeeper. But that's OK, because he's a great removal man.

'One Christmas,' he says, 'Nanna and Grandad were visiting from Scotland.'

I smile too because I know this one. It's about Pete and Danny when they were toddlers, thinking Nanna and Grandad's whisky was wee.

'Matt,' says Mum. 'What's wrong with your shoulder?'

Matt tries to look like nothing is, but the effort of pulling some crabgrass extra hard just made him wince.

'Let me see,' says Mum.

She pushes up the sleeve of his shirt.

Oh no.

A few hours ago it was just a scrape. Now Matt's shoulder is half covered with a huge bruise from where two hundred kilos of beef pronged him.

'It looks worse than it is,' mutters Matt.

Silently I ask the gods of soccer, the ones Uncle Cliff reckons players pray to before cup finals, to make a galah fly down and poo a seed on Mum's head so she gets distracted and doesn't ask how the bruise happened.

No galah appears. The gods of soccer must be English and don't know what a galah is.

Mum is still staring at the bruise. I can see she's getting upset.

Any mum probably would after what she's been through. Two and a half years ago, when we first got the news about the crash, we thought Matt was dead too.

'Matt,' says Mum. 'You promised you wouldn't play rough. How many times do I have to remind you? Your legs are held together by bits of metal.'

'Only three,' mutters Matt. 'Three tiny bits.'

Mum glares at him. They argue about this a lot.

It's not Mum's fault. When parents have kids that get killed, they end up extra anxious about their other ones. It's why I've got more asthma puffers than any other kid in my class. Including one that Mum hides in a tree on the corner of Bentley Street in case I run out on the way to school.

'Easy, love,' says Dad, putting his arm round Mum. 'It's only a bruise. It'll be gone in a week.'

'It's getting smaller already,' says Matt.

'It could be worse,' I say. 'My friend Shay, last week her big brother had an accident with a power sander and one of his tattoos got scraped off.'

Mum and Dad both look at me.

'It was only a stick-on one,' I say. 'But still.'

Mum laughs. One of those laughs that's almost

18

tearful. Then she sighs and the expression on her face is just like Gael-Anne gets after missing a goal. A mixture of upset and annoyed with herself.

'I'm sorry, Matt,' she says. 'I am trying.'

'You are, love,' says Dad.

We all know she is.

Uncle Cliff put it best. 'When your sons go off to a football match in the next town,' he said at the funeral, 'and for two of them the final whistle blows seventy years too early, and there's no extra time even when you beg, it's pretty hard to ever trust the ref again.'

I thought that was amazing. Uncle Cliff hasn't even got kids. And he used to be a ref in the under-six Sunday league.

Dad kisses Mum, then looks more closely at Matt's bruise.

'Hope the other bloke's is bigger,' he says.

Matt doesn't know what to say. We tell the truth in our family. But we also look after Mum.

'Let's get home,' says Dad. 'I need my tea.'

Me and Matt swap a relieved glance. No need for Mum to know about stampeding cattle. Except suddenly a thought plummets into my mind like a tree seed from the bum hole of a bird.

Those TV news cameras at the cattle yard, were any of them pointing at Matt?

5

No sign of Matt on the news.

So far.

On the TV, the visiting politician is telling the cattle-yard crowd about our beef going to China.

'Good news for a change,' says Mum.

I know why she's pleased. When our cattle go to China, they leave their skins behind. That means more leather for the leather goods factory where Mum works.

Dad nods, his mouth full.

Mum and Dad like to eat dinner while we watch the news. That way there's not too much chat and they don't miss the important stuff.

I pray Matt won't be on. If he is, Mum will definitely see it. She can cut a fish finger up and put it in her mouth without taking her eyes off the screen for a blink.

'Love, don't do that,' says Mum to Matt.

Matt's doing what he usually does when he sits on the settee. Flicking something from one foot to the other. Tonight it's a dirty sock.

'He's just practising,' I say. 'You need at least ten thousand hours of practice to get really good at anything. They've done studies.'

'And have they done studies,' says Dad, 'on how many hours of practice it takes to do what your parents tell you?'

Because he's Dad, he grins after he says it.

Matt stops flicking the sock.

I think the main reason Mum and Dad don't like Matt practising at dinner is it reminds us all of what he's lost. Before the accident everyone thought he'd be a professional soccer player one day. Now the doctors reckon his legs probably wouldn't stand the strain. We don't talk about it much, but we all know how disappointed Matt must be.

'What the . . . ?' says Dad.

Oh no.

Matt's on TV.

I've been dreading this, but I still have to look. What Matt did is even more amazing seeing it on TV. There are clouds of dust, but you can still see the cattle are trying to foul him the whole time. He doesn't lose his temper once. Or the ball.

I think the doctors are wrong.

If Matt's legs can survive that, they can survive anything.

'The Cristiano Ronaldo of the cattle yard,' says

the reporter. 'Showing the minister what fancy footwork really looks like.'

The segment ends. I peek at Mum. She's staring at the TV, her mouth open. I can see half-chewed fish finger, which she's always telling us we shouldn't ever let anyone see.

I hope she swallows it soon. Fish fingers can kill you if they get lodged in your airway. Asthma, page one.

'Judas H incredible,' says Dad.

Normally he'd be comforting Mum. But he's still staring at the TV.

I see why. The next segment's started. And it is incredible. Matt's in this one as well.

Franco Di Rafaela, one of the most famous footballers in the world, has just arrived in Australia for a year to play in the A League. Uncle Cliff reckons it's partly because he's a bit over the hill and partly because they're paying him millions.

This is his press interview at the airport. And one of the reporters is showing him a phone video of Matt in the cattle yard.

'Is this why you've come to Australia?' the reporter says to Franco Di Rafaela. 'So you can learn some new skills?'

Franco Di Rafaela frowns. He looks like he's hoping the reporter will be sent off. Then he shrugs in a weary but good-natured sort of way.

'Australia is a young country in football,' he says. 'I come here to be young again.'

He speaks good English, which isn't surprising. Everyone knows he's just spent a few years playing for a top English club.

He points to the reporter's phone, where a tiny Matt is still doing magic moves in the cattle yard.

'This boy is me,' says Franco Di Rafaela. 'Except I learned my football on the street. Much harder. Stampeding cattle are easy compared to the traffic in Italy.'

The reporters laugh. The segment ends.

We all look at each other, stunned. Except Mum, who leaves the room.

Looking upset. Really, really upset.

And angry.

'Matt,' she calls from her bedroom. 'Come in here, I want to talk to you.'

Matt looks at Dad.

Dad sighs, and signals for Matt to follow him into the bedroom. They both look like they're carrying about six wardrobes.

The phone starts ringing.

I'm the only one left, so I answer it.

'Bridie Sutherland,' I say. 'Sutherland residence.'

It's one of Mum and Dad's friends, telling them that Matt's just been on TV. I take a message. The phone rings again. And again. I take about twenty messages. I wish we had an answering machine, but Mum thinks they're rude.

Then Uncle Cliff comes crashing in through the screen door. He only lives in the next street, so

23

when he wants to tell us something he usually just comes over.

'How brilliant was that,' he says breathlessly. 'That was just totally Judas H brilliant.'

He sees it's just me in the room. He sees Mum and Dad aren't there.

His face changes.

I can see he's realising that maybe it wasn't totally Judas H brilliant for everyone.

6

I have the bad dream again.

The one I have a lot.

Me playing for Australia in a World Cup soccer final. Nil–nil with two minutes to go. I've got the ball. Matt wants me to pass to him.

But I can't kick.

There's bubble wrap round my legs. And my arms. And my chest.

Matt's not much better off. His soccer shirt and shorts are made of cotton wool. Which is growing like fungus.

It's over his head and feet now. He's being smothered in cotton wool.

The more I struggle to kick the ball, the tighter the bubble wrap gets.

Until I can't breathe. Or make a sound.

After that dream I can never get back to sleep, so I just lie here thinking about all the bad luck our family's had. And how it's about time we had some good luck.

Then I get up and creep through the dark house to the phone and ring information and get the number of the TV station who had Matt on their news.

7

Soon after it gets light, I hear Mum creep into Matt's room.

I can't hear everything through the wall, but I'm pretty sure she's saying sorry. For being a worry-guts. For making Matt suffer because of Pete and Danny. For trying to keep him wrapped up in cotton wool. I know that's probably what she's saying because I've heard her say it before, though I think last time she said bubble wrap.

Also, because she's a mum who's proud of what me and Matt do, she's probably saying well done for his footwork and the way he kept control of the ball when the cattle tried to tackle him from behind.

And she's probably also giving him a tickle and telling him not to get big-headed just because he's the first member of our family ever to be on TV.

So at breakfast I'm a bit surprised how stern she is.

'I don't want you running around today,' she says

to me and Matt. 'I want you at Uncle Cliff's.'

'Aw, Mum,' says Matt.

We're meant to be meeting the others. The orange lot want to do blindfold penalties again.

'I want someone keeping an eye on you both,' says Mum.

I'm outraged. Looking out for Matt is my job. One little incident in a cattle yard and people think you've lost it.

Plus it's only the second week of the school holidays. Are we going to spend the next three weeks at Uncle Cliff's? He's really nice, but he plays weird music.

I say that out loud.

'Probably only the next couple of days,' says Dad while Mum's putting on her work clothes. 'Try to understand.'

At Uncle Cliff's we spend the day helping him with housework and watching soccer on pay TV. Which makes more housework. Uncle Cliff gets very excited watching soccer on TV and biscuit crumbs go everywhere.

After my phone call last night, I'm really hoping we have some special visitors, but we don't. So instead I do a lot of thinking about how me and Matt can show Mum we don't need the cotton wool and the bubble wrap.

Late in the afternoon I have an idea.

'Uncle Cliff,' I say, 'can we sharpen your knives for you?'

If Mum hears we've done some dangerous things without getting hurt or bleeding to death, it'll show her we can look after ourselves.

Uncle Cliff peers at me, frowning, and I realise he can't hear me.

I go over to the sound system and turn down the music thudding out of the big speakers. It's Uncle Cliff's favourite group, the Rolling Stones. Except I'm surprised he still wants to listen to them after what he's been through lately.

'Can we sharpen your knives?' I say.

Uncle Cliff is fiddling with the vacuum cleaner. He's found some strands of Aunty Paula's hair tangled around the roller-brush attachment.

He answers without looking up.

'Thanks for the kind offer,' he says. 'But I haven't got a knife sharpener.'

I don't take it personally. Getting rid of sad memories must be a fiddly job when you're not used to using eyebrow tweezers.

'That power plug on the vacuum cleaner looks a bit dodgy,' says Matt, who's keeping one of Uncle Cliff's cushions up in the air just using his feet and head. 'Can I rewire it for you?'

Good old Matt. He understands my plan without me even telling him.

'No thanks,' says Uncle Cliff. 'It only looks a bit dodgy because it's off an old Xbox.'

I try to think of something else dangerous we can do.

'Do your gutters need a clean?' I say. 'Or your chainsaw?'

Uncle Cliff shakes his head, still fiddling with the roller-brush attachment.

I give Matt a look, hoping he'll think of something else. But he doesn't. He's still flipping the cushion.

Uncle Cliff gives a big sigh.

But it's not about the cushion. And I realise it's not about his knives or his gutters either.

Uncle Cliff is staring at the music system and he looks really sad.

He gets up and turns the music off.

I knew it was too soon for him to be listening to the Rolling Stones. Even though the song that was playing, 'I Can't Get No Satisfaction', is his all-time favourite. Aunty Paula only left him a few weeks ago. They went to see a Rolling Stones tribute band a couple of towns away, and the next day Aunty Paula emailed the pretend Mick Jagger and the rest is what Dad calls a king-size tragedy. He should know, he moves a lot of big beds.

Uncle Cliff sighs again.

'I need some fresh air,' he says, putting Aunty Paula's hairs into the kitchen bin. 'Let's go to the pub for tea.'

I glance at Matt to make sure he's still got his phone with him.

He has, which is good, because there might be a call coming through.

Really, as Matt's manager, I should have a phone of my own. So at moments like this, when arrangements change suddenly, people can still get hold of me.

8

Uncle Cliff knows Mr Daltry, the publican at the Horns And Tail Hotel, so me and Matt are allowed to have our tea sitting on boxes of crushed pear cider in the storeroom behind the bar.

That's good, because if any special visitors come looking for us, we can chat with them here in private.

Except it doesn't look like that's going to happen. Which is really disappointing. When I rang the TV station last night and told them Franco Di Rafaela should come and see Matt's talent in person, the man I spoke to was really friendly. He said he couldn't promise anything, but he congratulated me for doing such a good job as Matt's manager so late after my bedtime.

He must have changed his mind.

I'm glad now I didn't tell Matt I gave out his number. No point getting his hopes up when people can't tell the difference between a manager and a hoaxer.

Oh well, it was worth a try.

I put my plate down.

'I'm not really hungry,' I say.

Matt grunts and takes my steak. He doesn't like to talk while he's eating because it slows things down.

Through the half-open door I can see Uncle Cliff at the bar chatting with his mates. Behind him on the wall is a big-screen TV. The evening news is on. Suddenly so is our town. The main street and our school and the cattle yard. And a quick bit from yesterday of Franco Di Rafaela being annoyed at the airport.

'Look,' I say to Matt.

On the screen, Jayden and Zac and Celine and Gael-Anne are being interviewed by a reporter. So are some of the orange team. I can't hear the sound on the TV very well, but the orange kids are wiggling their hips a lot. I think they're trying to show the reporter Matt's dribbling style.

'Why didn't they interview you?' I say indignantly to Matt. 'You're the one they're talking about.'

'We've been at Uncle Cliff's,' says Matt. 'They wouldn't know where to find us.'

'They might have,' I say.

Everyone at the bar is looking at the TV. There's a quick picture of our house. Uncle Cliff and some of his friends give a cheer. Then the segment finishes and the newsreader comes back on.

'I pity footballers,' says Uncle Cliff to his mates. 'What's Rafaela, thirty-six? At least I got to forty-three before I was over the hill.'

The people at the bar have stopped listening to Uncle Cliff and are staring past him at something, their mouths open but no beer going in. Uncle Cliff doesn't notice.

'I must be the only bloke in this town,' he says gloomily, 'whose wife left him for an older man.'

People are nudging Uncle Cliff to be quiet.

Uncle Cliff turns to see what everyone is staring at. His face goes almost as stunned as it was the night he showed us Aunty Paula's goodbye note.

I know what's probably happened. A reporter has probably just walked in. He or she must have tracked Matt down at last. But not just any reporter. From the look on people's faces, it must be someone really famous.

Could it be the Channel Nine newsreader? While he's still on the screen? Is that possible?

I peek out of the storeroom.

Standing at the other end of the bar are three men, all wearing suits. Two of them I've never seen before, but the third one, who's shorter than the other two and has dark curly hair and slightly bandy legs, I recognise instantly.

Judas H incredible.

It's Franco Di Rafaela.

9

All the way home in Uncle Cliff's car, I try to keep calm.

Uncle Cliff doesn't.

'Rock 'n' roll, Matty,' he says. 'Franco Di Rafaela, here in person. I reckon it's because you remind him of when he was a kid. Probably wants a photo with you for his memoirs. They can be really emotional, Italian sports stars. He'll probably give you some signed boots. Or the ball he scored the winning goal with in the European Champions League final.'

Matt looks doubtful.

I don't say anything. I try to keep my thoughts calm and sensible, like a manager should.

The TV station must have passed my message on after all.

And now Franco Di Rafaela is here with a member of his management team and a marketing executive from his English club. And they didn't ask

Matt to do any skill at the pub, so they must already have made up their minds.

They're going to ask Matt to play for one of the best-known and most important soccer clubs in the world.

He'll be doing fast passing with some of the most famous players on the planet. I've seen them on TV. They're really rich and they don't go anywhere without their personal managers.

I glance at Matt.

His knees are jiggling like they do when he's excited. I can see he's having the same thoughts.

It must be incredible, to suddenly have your secret dream come true. The secret dream you've never told anybody except your sister years ago to take her mind off her chicken pox.

Matt grins at me.

I grin back.

Calm and sensible.

Calm and sensible.

10

Dad is hardly ever off balance.

I've seen him carry a glass-fronted china cabinet down some really steep steps in a thunderstorm and he didn't drop it once. Plus he had a toilet-brush under his arm.

But when me and Matt walk into our place with Franco Di Rafaela, Dad looks like he's going to fall off his chair.

Mum grips Dad's arm, but I think that's so she doesn't fall over either.

Everyone introduces themselves. The marketing executive from Franco Di Rafaela's English Premier League club is called Ken, and the member of his personal management team is called Bruno.

We all sit round the dining table, except Matt who prefers to stand. I sit next to Bruno so I can pick up managing tips.

Mum goes into the kitchen to make some tea.

Dad goes after her to get the biscuits.

'You have a very nice home,' says Ken to Matt.

'Thanks,' says Matt.

'Dad painted it last year,' I say. 'So if we have to sell the house in a hurry, we can.'

Everyone looks at me.

'Or we could just rent it out,' I say. 'If you need Matt to join the team straight away.'

Nobody says anything.

Matt goes out to the kitchen too. I don't think he can bear the excitement.

'Um,' says Ken, 'we might be having a slight misunderstanding here, Bridie. We haven't come to ask Matt to play for the club. Sorry.'

I stare at him.

'Why not?' I say.

A thought hits me. In the video, did they see the scars on Matt's legs? Is that what's putting them off?

No, it can't be that. Matt hasn't got that many scars. He just looks like a soccer player who's been kicked quite a bit.

'Matt is very talented,' says Franco Di Rafaela. 'But his size is not thick enough.'

'What Franco means,' says Ken, 'is that Matt has the wrong body shape for a modern professional footballer. He's too lightweight.'

This is crazy. They don't understand.

'I don't mean the first team,' I say. 'Not yet. I mean the youth team.'

The visitors all shake their heads.

'Still too lightweight,' says Ken apologetically. 'Matt is what's called an ectomorph. Lean and skinny. These days we find the young players that do best are mesomorphs. Chunky and strong.'

'Matt's only fourteen,' I say. 'He hasn't had his growth spurt yet.'

Ken sighs.

'The sad truth is,' he says, 'you can't ever change your body type.'

I don't believe him. That is so negative. I look at Bruno to see if he feels the same as me. Managers have to be positive, it's their job.

But Bruno is nodding sadly like he agrees with Ken.

I have one more go.

'What about Lionel Messi?' I say. 'He's the most famous footballer in the world and he isn't chunky.'

Nobody says anything.

I think they're trying to protect my feelings. Because now I think of it, as well as being short, Lionel Messi is quite chunky.

I want to plead and beg. Tell them talent is more important than chunkiness any day, plus I'll make Matt take vitamins.

But Mum and Dad come back in, and suddenly everyone's more interested in tea and biscuits.

I slump back in my chair. I'm so disappointed I don't hear what anyone else says for a bit. I can see lips moving, and Mum and Dad looking a bit stunned, but I don't take much in.

Outside I can hear a crowd murmuring. Half the pub followed us home. Uncle Cliff is out there keeping them quiet.

Dad's frowning like he's struggling to get his brain round something.

'Have I got this right?' he says to the visitors. 'You're offering to fly us all to England?'

'Exact,' says Franco Di Rafaela. 'We fly you free. Business class.'

'Come over and spend a few days with us at the club,' says Ken. 'Watch a match from the VIP box. Meet some famous players. All expenses paid.'

Mum and Dad look at each other.

I look at them both, my thoughts racing.

This actually isn't so bad. I've no idea why they're doing this, but once we're over there, Matt can show them in person that talent is more important than chunkiness.

'That's incredibly kind,' says Mum to Ken. 'But why us?'

'Fair question,' says Ken. 'Next week we're opening five superstores in Australia, all selling our club merchandise. While Franco's over here, he's helping us with the publicity. As part of that publicity we've been looking for an Australian family to take back to London as our guests. The media love that sort of thing. When we saw the coverage Matt's been getting for his party piece with the livestock, well, you lovely people are the obvious choice.'

Mum and Dad look at each other again.

Mum's face is doubtful.

Ken gives Franco Di Rafaela a quick glance.

Franco Di Rafaela turns to Matt, who's standing in the kitchen doorway, flipping an egg from one foot to the other and back again without breaking the shell. Mum usually yells at him, but she doesn't this time.

'What you think, Matt?' says Franco. 'Sounds fun, eh?'

After a moment or two, Matt nods.

'Of course,' says Ken, smiling, 'we're assuming you are a fan of our club.'

'Not really,' says Matt. 'I generally barrack for, you know, the less chunky clubs.'

He can be really witty, Matt, when he's paying attention.

The visitors all chuckle.

'It is a very kind offer,' says Dad. 'But we'd like to talk about it as a family. Can we give you an answer in the morning?'

The visitors glance at each other and nod.

I can see they understand. Our family is a team. In a team, everyone has a say.

Franco and the others don't have to worry. Once Mum and Dad and Matt realise what an opportunity this is, I know we'll all say yes.

11

After the visitors leave, Mum and Dad go to their room for a chat. Sometimes, before a team talk, parents like to have a parent talk.

I go to Matt's room for a manager talk.

Matt is lying on his bed, flipping his school lunchbox from foot to foot.

'They're right,' he says gloomily.

I want to shake him and tell him to snap out of it. But I don't. When a family's had a tragedy, it's normal for people to get a bit despairing, even after two soccer seasons.

'They're not right,' I say to Matt. 'OK, you're slim, but this is soccer, not heavyweight wrestling.'

'I don't mean that,' says Matt. 'I'm talking about what the surgeons told Mum. How if my legs get broken again, they can't put the pins back in and I'll be crippled.'

Sometimes Matt looks so worried I just want to

hug him. But you have to be careful of that with older brothers.

'Matt,' I say. 'Don't be a dope. Your legs have got skill, the best protection in the world. Look at those cattle. Did they hurt your legs? No, they didn't.'

Matt frowns and rubs his bruise.

'That's your shoulder,' I say. 'That's different.'

Matt doesn't look totally convinced.

'Anyway,' I say, 'when people see you play, I've never heard one person go, ooh look how fragile his legs are. And when people see how you can score goals, they almost poop themselves.'

Matt is still frowning, but a bit less.

'Your legs will be totally fine,' I say. 'Trust me.'

Sometimes managers have to say things, even if they're only ninety-nine percent sure. It's their job.

Matt grins.

'It would be Judas H incredible,' he says. 'Having a kick-around at a Premier League club.'

He flicks his school lunchbox in my direction.

I catch it on my knee. Matt's been teaching me a bit of ball and lunchbox control. Sometimes I think if I could run I'd be pretty good.

'It'll be more than a kick-around,' I say. 'Once we're there I reckon we can get you a try-out with the youth team. Dad's really ace at persuading people. Remember how he persuaded that woman not to put her tropical fish too close to her microwave?'

I flick the lunchbox back to Matt. Sort of. It clatters into his wardrobe.

Mum and Dad come in.

I see their faces and my chest goes tight.

'We're really sorry,' says Dad. 'We'd love to go to England, but we just can't do it.'

I'm struggling to breathe. Sometimes extreme disappointment can feel just like asthma.

'They want us to go in a week,' says Mum. 'But I haven't got holidays for months. If I take extra time off work, I could lose my job.'

'And even if Wal gives me time off,' says Dad, 'I can't leave Gran and Granpa.'

Oh no. I forgot about Gran and Granpa. They're so old they need help with everything on the farm. Sheep, chooks, fences, pills, everything. And Mum can't drive their old tractor, the fumes give her vertigo.

Frantically I try to think of a solution.

I can't.

'Which is why,' says Mum, 'you two will have to go without us.'

I stare at her.

'We know,' says Dad. 'Not what you were expecting.'

Mum takes a deep breath.

'Me and Dad have talked about it,' she says, 'and . . . well, there were a lot of things poor Pete and Danny didn't get to do, and there's no way anybody can fix that now, but we don't want to be the reason you two don't get to do things.'

I can see what a struggle it is for Mum to say

that, but I can also see she means it.

'I feel the same,' says Dad. 'We think it's time we started trusting that you can both stand on your own two feet.'

I open my mouth to tell them that we can, that we almost sharpened Uncle Cliff's knives and repaired his plug.

Then I remember we didn't.

So I just say thanks.

'This is a great chance for you both to see the world,' says Dad. 'And to have a squiz at some top-class European soccer. We'll probably never be able to afford to give you that chance ourselves, so we think you should grab it.'

'Thanks,' I say again, feeling a bit wobbly with the shock of it all. 'I promise I'll look after Matt.'

'And he'll look after you,' says Mum. 'Won't you, Matt?'

'Yeah,' says Matt. 'Course.'

But he's looking at me with a worried expression.

'I might need help,' he says to Mum and Dad.

'You'll have some,' says Dad.

He gives a whistle and a huge grin appears in the doorway. It's Mick Jagger's grin on Uncle Cliff's favourite Rolling Stones T-shirt, but inside it Uncle Cliff is grinning quite a lot as well.

'Rock 'n' roll, dudes,' he says. 'Last one to the airport's a bass player.'

First Half

12

When I was little and we still lived on the farm, it used to take ages to drive into town to my ballet class. Mum wouldn't go more than seventy Ks an hour. Fifty if I was doing leg-stretches in the back.

Flying to England takes even longer.

I keep wanting to say 'are we there yet' to Uncle Cliff, but he's watching an old rock concert with his headphones on. Next to him Ken is busy doing important Premier League marketing stuff on his computer, also with his headphones on. And next to me, Matt is fast asleep.

'Hello there,' says a voice.

I look up.

A lady has stopped by my seat. She's probably not a flight attendant because she's wearing yellow shorts and she's got an inflatable cushion round her neck.

'Poor little poppet,' she says. 'Why are you looking so miserable?'

I'm tempted to tell her how sad it was saying goodbye to Mum and Dad at the airport. How when they said 'see you in a week', all I could do was nod and hug them. How if things go well and Matt gets a contract with one of the world's most famous soccer clubs, we might not see them for months.

But I don't say anything because the lady doesn't give me the chance.

'There, there, it's not so bad,' she says, patting my arm. 'You're a very lucky girl, travelling in business class.'

I explain to her I'm in business class because I'm going to England on business.

'Wow,' she says. 'It must be extremely important business if they're sending a big girl like you to do it.'

I tell her I'm not that big really, only forty-seven kilos. Then I explain I'm Matt's manager and he's going to be a Premier League soccer star. And because the lady seems interested in business, I tell her Matt will probably earn two hundred thousand pounds. I also explain that pounds are like dollars, but worth more.

The lady chuckles like she knows something I don't.

'Your brother will be a very lucky boy,' she says, 'if he ends up earning two hundred thousand pounds a year.'

'Not a year,' I say. 'A week.'

The lady looks a bit stunned. People usually are when they find out how much top soccer players earn. Uncle Cliff reckons even the players go a bit faint sometimes.

I change the subject.

'Are you a ballerina?' I say, pointing to the lady's shoes, which are a bit like ballet ones.

The lady frowns. She is a bit plump to be a ballerina, and a bit old. I hope she doesn't think I'm being rude. I'm just trying to make conversation.

'I did ballet for two months,' I tell her. 'But Ms Creely the ballet teacher asked me to stop. She said I'd be better off doing rodeo. Which Mum said was a compliment.'

The lady opens her mouth, then closes it again.

'I'd better not talk any more,' I say. 'I don't want to wake my brother up. He's really tired.'

Which is true. On the way to the airport we had to go to the gala opening of one of the club superstores. Ken made us all pose for the TV cameras, and Matt got asked lots of questions by reporters. I could tell he found it exhausting, even though I answered most of them.

The lady pats my head and hurries away.

'You OK, Bridie?' says Uncle Cliff.

He's taken his headphones off and he leans towards me across the aisle.

'Are we there yet?' he whispers.

We both grin. And suddenly I want to confide

51

in him how I'm feeling a bit anxious. This is an incredible opportunity and everything, but I'm worried about Matt. The pressure on him. What if the leg pains he had last year come back? When he's got them, he doesn't even like going to school, let alone England.

Uncle Cliff listens carefully. He nods and you feel he really understands. He must have been a great person to take a faulty toaster back to.

'You're right,' he says. 'It is a big responsibility for Matt.'

'But luckily,' says a voice on the other side of me, 'I've got a really good manager.'

I turn round.

Matt is awake.

'And a fairly good uncle,' he says.

We all grin.

Suddenly I don't feel anxious any more. I'm remembering how brave and determined Matt can be. When I was three he saved me from a snake. It was only a jelly one, but still. I was choking and he reached into my mouth and pulled it out with his bare hands. There was sick in there and everything.

Matt goes back to his usual expression, which is serious.

'I want to do it for Mum and Dad,' he says. 'They've worked their bums off for years and years to give us a good life, including weekends. And look what life gave them. So they deserve some good stuff.'

I nod.

I'm feeling too emotional to say anything, so I just give Matt a look. So he can see I'm feeling the same as him.

Millions of pounds won't bring back what our family's lost, but at least Mum and Dad won't have to work overtime any more.

We'll do it.

If it's humanly possible, we will.

Uncle Cliff gives us both a high-five.

'Team Sutherland,' he says, which is very generous because his name's McGuffin.

I glance across at Ken. He's still on his laptop with his headphones on. Pity he's missing this. He's probably still thinking of Matt as just a photo opportunity. Rather than a match-winning goal-scoring genius.

The flight starts to be more fun, even with fifteen hours to go.

First me and Matt and Uncle Cliff make a list of all the famous footballers we hope Matt will play with. Because that means we'll meet them.

Then we stretch our legs at Singapore airport, which has about a hundred kilometres of carpet. We find a quiet bit, and Matt and Uncle Cliff have a kick-around with a business-class toilet bag.

Back on the plane we discover that the entertainment system has some really good soccer matches, and me and Matt work out how to get football on our screens and relaxing music on our headphones at the same time.

I doze a bit. Whenever I open my eyes there are beautiful midfield build-ups on the screen, all elegant and flowing like when Dad unpacks a four-bedroom house.

Each time someone scores a goal, I imagine it's Matt.

Because soon it will be.

13

If you ever fly to England, try to have a top Premier League soccer club do all the travel arrangements.

They're really thoughtful. They get everyone a passport and give your uncle special elastic socks so his ankles don't swell up on the plane. And when you get to London airport they have a big car waiting with a driver.

Ken gets in the front, and me and Matt and Uncle Cliff sit in the back and just stare at the TV screens and leather seats and the strips of shiny luxury wood on the inside of the doors. I've never seen wood in a car before, except on our way home from the hardware store.

Then we all fall asleep. (Not the driver.)

When we wake up, Ken is leaning over from the front seat shaking Uncle Cliff's knee.

'Wakey, wakey,' he's saying. 'Here's your digs.'

That must be English for hotel.

I peer out the car window. I can't see a hotel. Or a motel or even a caravan park. We're in a street completely full of old-looking houses. Tall ones all joined together.

The car stops outside a house with a dark green hedge in front of it. The top of the hedge has been clipped into unusual shapes.

'Judas H amazing,' says Uncle Cliff. 'Soccer balls.'

'Everybody out,' says Ken. 'Come and meet Mrs Jarvis.'

Outside the car it's freezing. Ken warned us about this before we left. Luckily our local charity shop had some old ski clothes. I zip my jacket up and make sure Matt's scarf is tucked in all round his neck. I can see Matt wishes he was wearing an old leather motorbike jacket like Uncle Cliff instead of a tangerine ski parka.

As we go through the gate, the front door opens. A pretty lady with short dark hair smiles at us. She mustn't feel the cold because she's only wearing a white shirt and jeans.

'Come in,' she says. 'Make yourselves at home.'

Inside the house it's warm. We take our coats off and introduce ourselves to Mrs Jarvis.

'Nice hair,' she says to Uncle Cliff.

I've never seen Uncle Cliff blush before. He's very proud of his hair. Specially the little blue feathers I gave him for his birthday.

'Keith Richards,' says Mrs Jarvis.

That's the name of Uncle Cliff's favourite person in the Rolling Stones.

Uncle Cliff beams, and I can see he's feeling at home already.

Mrs Jarvis takes us into a room with a fire burning in a fireplace and a table covered with breakfast things.

'Bacon and eggs for everyone?' she says.

While she goes to get it, Ken explains that a lot of the youth academy boys from overseas live in digs like Mrs Jarvis's place. So their health and diet and bedtimes can be supervised by specially trained people like Mrs Jarvis.

I look around the room. It's different to an Australian room. The ceiling is really high up. Probably so the youth academy kids, when the weather's bad, can practise headers indoors.

Ken also explains that we're staying here instead of in a hotel because it's got better photo opportunities for the media. Makes us look like we're part of the club family.

'Which you are,' says Ken. 'For example, today one of our club's most famous players has invited you to his place for afternoon tea.'

Ken says the famous player's name, but I'm not going to repeat it because a good manager respects privacy.

But you'd know it.

My head is buzzing, partly because I'm very sleepy and partly at the thought of meeting such a huge star in person. If anyone can give Matt hints about how to get into the team, he'll be able to. And tell Matt what type of wallet is best when you earn two hundred thousand pounds a week.

Mrs Jarvis comes back with a tray of bacon and eggs.

'Pop this into you,' she says. 'Then you can have a little snooze before your outing this afternoon.'

She smiles at Matt.

'At least you won't have any trouble getting to sleep,' she says. 'Not like the other poor loves I've had staying here. Those academy boys get so stressed about impressing the club I have to put them on a hot milk drip.'

'Sounds very nice,' says Uncle Cliff. 'You can hook me up any time.'

Mrs Jarvis gives him a look.

'It's a figure of speech, Cliff,' she says. 'If you put somebody on a hot milk drip their blood coagulates and they go into vascular trauma.'

'Sorry,' says Uncle Cliff.

'Anyway,' says Mrs Jarvis, looking more cheerful. 'This is nice. You're here on a fun holiday without a care in the world, and you can just relax.'

After she goes out to get more toast, me and Matt swap a look.

If only she knew how wrong she was.

14

I've read a few soccer star biographies, and they usually have stuff that makes ordinary people jealous. Humungous houses and million-dollar cars and hat-tricks at Wembley and cures for asthma in very expensive spa resorts.

There's a bit of that here in the soccer star's house where we've come for afternoon tea.

A waterfall, for example. Indoors. On purpose, not just because a toilet's blocked upstairs.

And a lift.

And a cinema.

And a swimming pool in the basement.

'Judas H amazing,' says Uncle Cliff, staring up at the waterfall.

A phone on the wall buzzes.

The soccer star's wife picks it up, listens to it, and presses a button. She grabs a remote, opens the blinds and peers out of one of the huge windows.

In the distance, a car is coming up the very long driveway.

'Media's here,' says the soccer star's wife, checking her reflection in a shiny painting.

She doesn't need to worry. She looks very beautiful. Specially her hair, which is even more carefully done than Uncle Cliff's.

Ken, who brought us here, heads towards the door.

'I'll go and meet them, Terrine,' he says to the soccer star's wife. 'Just a bit of filming. Won't take long, I promise.'

Terrine looks around the big living room.

'Where's Gazz?' she says, sounding a bit annoyed.

I'm not sure who Gazz is. Her dog? Her personal assistant? Then I realise it must be her nickname for her soccer star husband. I don't know why she calls him that. His name isn't Garry, or Gareth, or Garibaldo. Well, maybe his middle name is.

'I bet he's out on that blessed pitch,' says Terrine.

She presses another button on the remote, and more blinds open on the other side of the room.

'Judas H,' says Uncle Cliff. He's so stunned he can't even finish the sentence. I know how he feels.

Outside, right next to the house, is a soccer pitch. Not a normal backyard one with a garden path down one side and a clothes hoist in the middle.

A full-size one.

With full-size goals.

And floodlights.

And hundreds of balls all over it.

Up one end a man in a silver tracksuit is taking penalties. One after another. Banging them in. It doesn't look too hard because there's no goalie. Standing in the goal there's just a statue that looks ancient Greek or something.

'Come and meet Gazz,' says Terrine.

We walk across the pitch, which is made of real grass. As we get closer, Gazz, or as you would know him, one of the most famous footballers in the world, turns and looks at us.

''Allo,' he says. 'Who are you?'

It really is him. I'm feeling a bit faint and I can't actually speak. I can see Matt and Uncle Cliff are the same.

'Ken brought them,' says Terrine. 'Superstores in Australia, remember?'

'Oh, yeah,' says Gazz. 'Wotcha.'

While we all struggle to say g'day, Gazz drags the statue out of the goal.

'You play?' he says to Uncle Cliff.

'Just a bit of drums,' mumbles Uncle Cliff.

Gazz gives him a look, then chuckles.

'Shame,' he says. 'Elton John was here last week.'

I take a deep breath and try to stay calm. My heart wants to leap out of my chest and do joyful cartwheels down the pitch. Not because of Elton John. Because I've just noticed something.

Gazz isn't that chunky.

He's more muscly than Matt, but in no way is

he mega-chunky. So it is possible to be a Premier League star without being two hundred kilos of beef.

'My brother Matt plays soccer,' I say. 'He's very good.'

'Is that right?' says Gazz, looking at Matt. 'Alright nipper, in goal.'

I start to explain that Matt isn't really a goalie, but Gazz dribbles a ball away down the pitch. Matt goes in goal. Gazz does a few shots. Matt throws himself at each ball, but they all get past him.

'Good try,' says Gazz to Matt each time.

'He's not really a goalie,' I say.

But Gazz doesn't hear me. He's distracted by Ken arriving with the media, who are a man with a video camera and a woman with a microphone on a pole.

'This is for Australian TV,' Ken explains to Gazz.

'Righty-o,' says Gazz. 'We'd better see our Aussie in action then.' He turns to Matt. 'Me in goal, you on penalties.'

'Actually,' says Matt, 'can I do some long shots?'

'Knock yourself out,' says Gazz, jiggling up and down between the goal posts and giving Ken a wink.

Matt pulls his phone out of his jeans pocket and hands it to me. He always does that when he's planning to do some big kicks.

He takes a ball halfway towards the middle of the pitch. Then he turns and shoots. The ball misses the goal by miles.

'Sorry,' says Matt.

I think his legs might be a bit stiff after the flight. Metal leg pins can do that. But I don't say anything. If the club finds out he's got metal in his legs, even a tiny bit, they might not give him a fair go.

'He's nervous,' I say to Gazz. 'We've never played with goal nets before.'

'Come closer,' calls Gazz to Matt. 'Give yourself a chance.'

Matt moves a ball two steps closer to the goal and shoots. Gazz doesn't move. He doesn't think he needs to. Then he realises he should have done. The ball's in the back of the net.

'Woah,' says Gazz to Uncle Cliff. 'What you been feeding him?'

Uncle Cliff thinks about this.

'Bacon and eggs,' he says. 'And we had some pork and pistachio paté on the plane.'

'Shall I do more?' says Matt, lining up another ball.

'Bring it on,' says Gazz, really concentrating now, crouching and flexing his shoulders.

Matt does six more shots. Gazz does some really spectacular dives, but he doesn't touch the ball once.

I'm hoping that with each goal Matt scores, Gazz will be more and more impressed. It's not working out that way. He's getting more and more irritated.

Gazz picks himself up for the sixth time and rubs his neck.

'We need a new bed,' he says to Terrine. 'That water bed's doing my back in.'

Terrine doesn't look like she agrees. I need to be a manager quickly.

'I know,' I say. 'Let's play blindfold penalties.'

Ken frowns.

'I think we've got enough on video,' he says, looking nervously at Gazz.

'Blindfold penalties?' says Gazz. 'I haven't played that since I was nine.'

'This has been lovely,' says Ken. 'Thanks for having us, Terrine. We'll get out of your hair now.'

'Hang on,' says Gazz. 'Few more minutes won't hurt.'

Ken gives in. Me and Matt and Gazz show the others how blindfold penalties work. After a bit, Terrine wants a go. And the cameraman.

We play it for ages and have lots of fun.

Then, after Terrine scores a hat-trick and does a bit of dancing around, she looks at her watch.

'Blimey,' she says. 'We're late for drinks with the Beckhams.'

Suddenly everyone is saying goodbye and packing up.

This is my last chance.

'Excuse me,' I say to Gazz. 'Do you think Matt's good enough to play in the Premier League? You know, one day?'

Gazz doesn't say anything at first. He looks over at Matt like Matt's a new waterfall he's just installed and he's not sure about.

'Got talent,' says Gazz. 'But scouting isn't really

my area. Best talk to the people at the academy.'

'Let's go there now,' I say to Ken, in a voice that is perhaps a bit too pushy for a visitor.

Ken shakes his head.

'We've done enough for today,' he says.

Gazz frowns thoughtfully.

'Few shots at the youth academy wouldn't be bad,' he says. 'Give you more, you know, like, you know . . .'

'Visual variety,' says the cameraman.

'Yeah,' says Gazz.

I don't exactly know what that means, but I can see Ken does, because he sighs.

'Alright,' says Ken. 'But we'll have to make it quick.'

I've never met Gazz before. I don't know him personally at all. And ordinary people like me are meant to keep our distance from big stars.

So I don't give him a hug.

But if things work out like I'm hoping, and in a few years I write Matt's soccer star biography, I'm going to give Gazz a very big thank you.

15

*I*n the car on the way to the training centre, Matt is very quiet.

'You OK?' I say.

'I want to get Mum and Dad a house like that,' Matt says. 'With a waterfall.'

I look at him.

He means it. I feel a jab of worry. I don't think we should be planning a new house just yet. Not without checking with Mum and Dad.

'Waterfalls probably take a lot of looking after,' I say.

'In a drought,' says Uncle Cliff, 'you'd have to use lemonade.'

Matt doesn't say anything. I think he knows Uncle Cliff is joking. Maybe not.

'There are only four of us,' I say. 'So we wouldn't really need nine bedrooms.'

'And a six-car garage is a bit of a waste,' says

Uncle Cliff. 'Unless your dad gets his own removal truck and wants to park it on its side.'

Matt still doesn't say anything. Which is not like him. He's not the chattiest person in the world, but he usually can't resist having a go at Uncle Cliff when Uncle Cliff's being a prawn.

I'm tempted to give Matt a tickle. Just to relieve the stress. But before I can, we arrive at the training centre.

It's huge.

We all gape through the car window.

There are loads of modern buildings and loads and loads of soccer pitches.

'OK,' says Ken from the front seat. 'Quick tour, bit of video for the media, then back to Mrs J's. You lot must be exhausted. I know I am.'

I am a bit. But I don't care. Because on some of the pitches are exactly what I hoped would be there.

Boys playing football. Academy kids showing what they're made of. And loads of trainers watching them, trying to decide if they're good enough to get into the first team one day.

Just seeing them makes my heart do a step-over.

That's where Matt should be.

Ken is right. The tour is quick. We see offices and changing rooms and classrooms and gyms and rooms full of computers and screens. We also see a full-size soccer pitch completely indoors.

'Wonder if Gazz and Terrine know about this?' says Uncle Cliff. 'They could do a patio extension.'

It's a good thought, but I don't really care about patio extensions at the moment. I can only think about one thing. I know Matt is thinking the same. Every time we pass a window, we gaze out at the boys playing on the training pitches.

'I think we've got everything we need,' says Ken to the cameraman.

Before the cameraman agrees and we all get whisked back out to the car, I make a suggestion.

'Why don't you film Matt playing in a game?' I say. 'It'd be great visual variety.'

The cameraman thinks about this. I hope I got the words right.

'She's not wrong,' says the cameraman to Ken. 'It would be.'

Ken looks like a person who just wants to go home and go to bed.

'Matt hasn't got any boots,' he says. 'You can't play on a training pitch without boots. And the kit room's closed for the day.'

I unzip my Loch Ness Monster backpack and take out Matt's soccer boots and shorts. No way are we going anywhere on this trip without them.

Matt and Uncle Cliff give me grateful grins.

I feel a bit guilty about keeping Ken up. But sometimes, when her brother's dream is at stake, a manager has to be ruthless.

16

As we hurry towards the under-fifteen training pitch, I start to get a feeling in my tummy that something isn't right.

It's the right game, soccer.

And there's skill all over the place. Which is perfect for Matt because he won't have to get into any arguments about changing sides.

And the pitch looks brilliant. Smooth and green and completely free of wombat activity.

And yet something's a bit weird.

Is it the gloomy weather? It's afternoon, but the sky is sort of dark and it feels like dusk is coming. English people must have good eyes because the boys on the pitch can obviously see the ball, judging by the clever things they're doing with it.

Then the floodlights snap on and I blink a few times and see what's strange.

The boys playing all have grim faces. So do the

trainers. The other adults standing along the edge of the pitch are looking very serious too. They must be parents because they aren't watching the whole game, just keeping their eyes clamped on their own kids.

Nobody is laughing, whooping, making jokes, rolling their eyes, howling with joy or tickling each other in the way that soccer is normally played.

Of course. It must be the cameras.

There's other videoing going on apart from our cameraman. The club is doing it too, with cameras set up on each side of the pitch.

It's a known fact that people can be a bit stiff and serious when cameras are pointing at them. Look at politicians.

Ken is speaking to one of the trainers and pointing at Matt. The trainer stares at Matt for a moment. Then he nods.

'This is it,' says Uncle Cliff. 'Rock 'n' roll.'

The trainer yells at one of the boys on the pitch, who trots grumpily over, takes off his coloured team bib and holds it out to Matt.

'Thanks,' says Matt, taking it and putting it on.

The boy doesn't reply. Just scowls at Matt.

'Don't take it personally,' I say to the boy. 'Matt'd do the same for you.'

The trainer has a word to Matt, and Matt runs onto the pitch to a midfield position. I can see from his lips moving that he's saying g'day to a couple of the other boys.

They don't reply. Maybe in England you have to be introduced first.

The game starts up again. I see that me and Uncle Cliff aren't the only people who know about fast passing. This is the fastest passing I've ever seen. But there's something strange about it. Passing is to stop you being tackled. Half the time these kids bash into each other anyway.

Nobody passes to Matt.

'Come on,' yells Uncle Cliff. 'He's a visitor.'

Matt doesn't wait for people to be kind. He starts getting the ball himself and passing it around. Except sometimes he doesn't because sometimes, as soon as he gets the ball, other boys bash into him and knock him over.

'Hey ref,' yells Uncle Cliff, 'fair go.'

The ref obviously doesn't know what that means because he hardly ever blows the whistle.

Me and Uncle Cliff look at each other anxiously.

I can see we're both thinking the same thing.

Leg pins.

'Use your skill,' I yell at Matt.

'And remember there's no Medicare over here,' yells Uncle Cliff.

Matt gets the ball again. A big kid who's already knocked Matt over a couple of times slides at him. Matt leans back and glides past. Just like Dad getting a flat screen TV past a bulky armchair.

'Go Matt,' I yell. 'Good skill.'

Uncle Cliff does some encouraging whoops.

Some of the parents are frowning at us. Maybe there's some sort of academy rule banning encouraging whoops.

Matt steers a great pass through three defenders to a team-mate who can't miss.

'Goal!'

Me and Uncle Cliff are the only ones who yell it.

Nobody else makes a sound. It was a goal but they don't clap or look happy or anything. Not the players or the trainers or the parents.

This really is weird. Maybe no cheering for a goal is also an academy rule.

Then something else happens I've never seen before. Matt goes back to the big kid, who's still on the ground after the missed tackle, and holds out a hand to help him up. The big kid scowls and knocks Matt's hand away and gets up by himself.

I'm shocked and I can see Matt is too.

All I can think of is that the big kid comes from a part of the world where helping people up is rude. He looks like he might be African. But I've seen African people in movies helping each other quite a lot.

The game starts again and I can see Matt is struggling with the shock. For a while he hangs back and doesn't go for the ball.

Then suddenly he does.

He gets the ball and takes it past about six players and shoots from a long way out.

Me and Uncle Cliff stay quiet this time.

Everyone else is quiet too. They're experiencing shock now. People just stare at Matt, and at the ball spinning in the back of the net.

The game doesn't go on for much longer. After a while one of the trainers yells for everyone to get changed. As the players come off the pitch, their parents go over to them. But there's not a lot of congratulations or hugs.

The most enthusiastic adult is Uncle Cliff. He does a high-five. Matt does a small one back.

'Are you OK?' I say to him anxiously.

Matt nods and flops onto the ground to take his boots off.

I rub his legs.

'We won't tell Mum about the rough tackles,' I say to him.

'Don't worry,' says Uncle Cliff. 'I'll tell the Aussie media not to show those bits back home.'

He heads over towards Ken and the cameraman.

'You were Judas H amazing,' I say to Matt. 'Are you sure you're OK? Can you feel both your legs?'

Matt gives me a look. I can see he doesn't want me making a fuss of him in front of everyone.

I back off.

One boy is leaving the pitch on his own. It's the big kid who knocked Matt's hand away. I guess it makes sense he's on his own. If he comes from a far-off place like Africa, his parents probably aren't able to be here.

I know what that feels like.

I go over to him.

'Excuse me,' I say. 'Matt was just trying to be friendly.'

The boy stares at me blankly.

'We help people in Australia,' I say. 'It's one of the things we do. You know, like suck their leg if they've been bitten by something.'

The boy sighs.

'Help someone in this place,' he says quietly, 'and you kill them.'

I stare at him as he walks away.

I may not be the smartest person in the world. For example I can have trouble with poetry and car manuals. But usually I get stuff.

Not at the moment.

I haven't got a clue what that boy meant.

17

People in soccer star biographies mostly spend their time in luxury hotels and private jets and lounge rooms where you need a personal hairdresser to stop your hair going flat from the waterfall mist. They don't spend much time at all in training-centre corridors with nowhere to sit down.

The only reason me and Matt and Uncle Cliff are here is Ken.

'Cool your heels for a bit,' he says, and disappears.

'I reckon he needs the loo,' whispers Uncle Cliff. 'That amazing goal of yours, Matt. Must have got his bladder in a twist. Did mine.'

Matt grins.

I hear a door open and glance over. And see something that gets my bladder in a twist.

The African boy who rejected Matt's help is striding towards us with a determined face. As he gets closer he lifts his hand.

For a moment I think he's going to whack Matt. I get ready to throw myself at him and hope Uncle Cliff will back me up. Uncle Cliff's got several skull rings that would be pretty scary in a fight.

But the African boy just wants Matt to do one of those up in the air handshakes. Like a high-five but with twisty bits.

Matt does it, a bit uncertain.

'Ayo,' says the boy.

Matt looks even more uncertain.

'Ayodele Awolopo,' says the boy.

It's his name. I check the spelling with him. And do the handshake.

'Sorry, man,' says Ayo to Matt. 'Didn't mean to be rude out there. Forgot you was a visitor.'

'S'OK,' says Matt. 'Thanks.'

Uncle Cliff has his arm up too. Ayo does the handshake with him.

'You weren't the only one who forgot,' says Uncle Cliff. 'I reckon they all did, ref included.'

'No, no,' says Ayo. 'They didn't forget. He got royal family treatment, this boy.'

We look at Ayo, puzzled.

'No he didn't,' I say. 'They knocked Matt over about ten times.'

'Bit of biff, very normal,' says Ayo. 'You should see the things they didn't do.'

'Like what?' says Uncle Cliff.

Ayo hesitates. He glances up and down the corridor like he doesn't want anyone to see, then he takes a couple of steps closer to Matt.

'Give you an example,' he says. 'We're in the penalty area, right?' He points to Uncle Cliff. 'He's the ref.'

'Which he was,' I say. 'Under-sixes.'

'First thing,' says Ayo to Matt, 'I turn you.'

Before Matt can say anything, Ayo grabs Matt's hips and suddenly Matt is between Ayo and Uncle Cliff.

'Now I'm behind you,' says Ayo. 'So you're blocking the ref's vision of what I'm doing to you.'

'What are you doing to him?' I say.

'Jump,' says Ayo to Matt.

Matt tries to jump, but his feet don't leave the ground because Ayo is holding two fistfuls of Matt's jacket really tight.

Ayo lets go.

'Go for the ball,' he says.

Matt tries to move away as if he's going for the ball. Ayo does a little movement, you can hardly see it, but his knee goes in behind Matt's and suddenly Matt is on the ground.

Ayo helps him up.

I'm horrified. I've never seen cheating like this. Matt is looking pretty unhappy too.

'Where are you from?' says Uncle Cliff indignantly to Ayo.

'Nigeria,' says Ayo.

'And this is what they teach you in Nigeria?' says Uncle Cliff.

'No,' says Ayo. 'It's what they teach us here.'

We look at him, stunned.

I can't believe it. This is one of the most famous soccer clubs in the world. I've seen them play on TV heaps and I've never seen them doing cheating like this.

Is Ayo making all this up? Or is this something else they teach here, how to hide cheating from the TV cameras?

I take a deep breath and tell myself to calm down. I'm a manager. A manager's job is to stay positive and help lifelong dreams come true.

At least Ayo's being friendly, showing us all this stuff. And it might just be stuff that's reserved for special occasions, like being six–nil down in an FA Cup Final.

'Ah,' says a voice. 'There you are, Ayo. Your lift is waiting.'

The voice belongs to a man in a tracksuit. He's walking towards us along the corridor with Ken.

Ayo looks at the man nervously.

'Nice to meet you,' Ayo mutters to us, and hurries away.

Ken introduces us all.

'This is Neal Merchant,' he says. 'The head coach here at the academy.'

Good. Exactly the person who can confirm that all the stuff Ayo's shown us is only to be used in emergencies.

'Excuse me,' I say to Mr Merchant.

But he doesn't hear me. All his attention is on Matt.

'So, Matt,' he says. 'The under-fifteen trainers have told me good things about you. Very good things. And we'd like to make you an offer. For the remainder of your week here, we'd like you to join our training program.'

I can see Uncle Cliff struggling not to whoop.

'What do you say?' Mr Merchant asks Matt.

Matt glances down the corridor, in the direction Ayo went.

Uncle Cliff is nodding at Matt, urging him to say yes.

I start nodding at him too.

But Matt's the one who has to answer. The offer was made to him. It's his dream.

He says yes.

18

We're all glowing with happiness in the car going back to Mrs Jarvis's.

'Yee-ha,' says Uncle Cliff. 'You're on your way, Matty.'

My doubts are on their way too. On their way to disappearing.

Today was Matt's first day and first days are always a bit weird. It's like my first day at primary school. The year twos made us new kids use the toilet near the ants nest. It was called the tickle toot. I reckon that's probably what Ayo and the others were doing just now on the pitch. Giving Matt a taste of the tickle toot.

'You're a lucky boy, Matt,' says Ken as he steers us through the traffic. 'Do you know how many kids round the world dream of training with a club like ours?'

Uncle Cliff thinks about this.

'Is the number more than fifty thousand or less than fifty thousand?' he says.

Ken laughs.

'Millions,' he says.

'Hear that, Matt,' I say. 'You're one in a million.'

As Matt's manager and somebody who's not very good at maths, I'm allowed to exaggerate a bit.

Nobody in the car disagrees with me, and that's the toast Uncle Cliff makes back at Mrs Jarvis's.

'To our one-in-a-million kid,' he says.

We all clink our teacups.

Ken says he won't stay for dinner.

After he goes, Mrs Jarvis serves up a delicious lamb hotpot.

'This is top tucker,' says Uncle Cliff to Mrs Jarvis. 'I could eat this three times a day.'

'That wouldn't be a good idea, Cliff,' says Mrs Jarvis. 'Your digestive system would get over-stressed and you'd end up with a spastic colon.'

Uncle Cliff doesn't seem to mind. Probably because Mrs Jarvis is so pretty.

I know I should let the grown-ups talk more. Mrs Jarvis is single like Uncle Cliff. Her husband is living with a sports physiotherapist in Gdansk.

But there's something I have to ask.

'Mrs Jarvis,' I say. 'Today we met a boy at the youth academy called Ayo.'

She pauses in the middle of giving Uncle Cliff another dollop of hotpot.

'Ayodele Awolopo,' she says, smiling. 'Sweet boy.

And a very good player. The top kid in the under-fifteens.'

I tell Mrs Jarvis what Ayo said. How if you help somebody at the academy, you kill them.

Matt and Uncle Cliff frown. They haven't heard about this.

'What did Ayo mean?' I ask Mrs Jarvis.

She sighs.

'It's so competitive at the academy,' she says. 'They're all terrified. They think if they look weak or vulnerable, they'll miss out.'

I don't understand.

'But Ayo's been chosen,' I say. 'The club's chosen him to train with them. He's made it.'

'That's only the start,' says Mrs Jarvis. 'Out of all the boys training there, do you know how many actually make it into the first team and earn the big money?'

I look at Matt and Uncle Cliff.

None of us know.

'Is the number more than fifty or less than fifty?' says Uncle Cliff.

'Some years it's none,' says Mrs Jarvis.

We stare at her.

'Some years it's one,' she says. 'Two tops. Same with all the big clubs. And do you know the crazy thing? After they've ditched most of their academy trainees, they pay huge money to buy players from other clubs.'

We sit there in silence, taking this in.

Matt is looking stunned.

Uncle Cliff's mouth is hanging open. I can see half-chewed hotpot. Which looks even more of a risk to your breathing than half-chewed fish finger.

I'm finding it a bit hard to breathe myself.

I get it now. The reason the academy boys are so grim and rough and not interested in having fun.

They're all desperate to be the one.

What are they going to do when they find out the one is Matt?

19

Before we go to bed, we Skype Mum and Dad on Uncle Cliff's laptop, and tell them about Matt being invited to train with the club for the rest of the week.

'Wow,' says Mum.

'Not surprising,' says Dad. 'Good on you, Matt.'

But then Mum and Dad glance at each other, and I can see what they're thinking.

Leg pins.

'Be careful, love,' says Mum to Matt. 'Have fun, but take it easy.'

'Don't worry,' I say to Mum. 'The other boys are giving Matt the royal family treatment,'

Uncle Cliff helps Mum feel better too. He tells her and Dad about the photos he's put on Facebook.

'It's everything we've been doing,' he says.

That isn't totally true. There are lots of photos of the pork and pistachio paté and Mrs Jarvis's hedge and Gazz's waterfall and the training centre and Mrs Jarvis, but Uncle Cliff has very kindly made sure for Mum's sake that there isn't a single photo of a grim face or a rough tackle.

Mum and Dad relax a bit.

Sort of.

After we all go to bed, I creep into Matt's room.

I knock first. It's best with older brothers, even in digs.

'Yo,' he says.

I go in. His lamp is on and he's lying on top of the bed in his pyjamas, bouncing a rolled-up sock between his knees.

'Can't you sleep either?' says Matt.

He sits up and I sit next to him.

'Mum and Dad were feeling really proud of you,' I say.

Matt nods, but doesn't say anything.

We both know Mum and Dad were feeling a lot of other things too.

'You can be the one, Matt,' I say. 'I know you can. David Beckham signed with Manchester United when he was fourteen. No way is he chunkier than you, and I reckon you're more determined than him. And more talented.'

We look at each other.

I can see Matt is having worried thoughts. Probably about leg pins.

I try not to let him see the thoughts I'm suddenly having.

Does this mean we won't see Mum and Dad for a long time? Does it mean I'll have to leave school? I'm not even sure if that's legal at ten.

Matt puts his arm round me.

Which is a surprise. He doesn't do that much these days.

I want to snuggle into him and let him cuddle me. But I don't. Right now he doesn't need a soppy little sister, he needs a manager.

Matt is frowning. I know he's thinking about Mum and Dad. About how tired they looked tonight. About how much they need a long rest. Ideally in a big comfortable house with automatic blinds.

I've never seen Matt look quite like this before.

He definitely is more determined than David Beckham.

20

I'm glad Mum isn't at Matt's first training session. I'm glad she's on the other side of the planet in bed. Not having to see what Matt's doing.

I can hardly look myself.

The trainers made the boys pair off and take turns to keep the ball away from each other. Matt chose Ayo. I would too. He's the only kid who's been even a bit friendly.

Big mistake.

Matt started with the ball, and Ayo slammed into him like a fridge on castors. That happened to Dad once, on a sloping driveway. But Dad was able to go to hospital. He didn't have to pick himself up and try to get a ball back from the fridge.

'Fair go,' yells Uncle Cliff.

We're standing at the edge of the pitch, jiggling up and down, partly to keep warm and partly because we're so indignant about what's going on.

Nobody else seems to mind. A few other parents are just standing around watching. They don't look very happy, but that's probably because the weather's so bleak and grey. Even the trees around here are shivering. None of them have got any leaves and the only birds you ever see in them are those big black English ones that make tragic sounds.

Ayo is kicking at Matt's ankles while Matt dribbles the ball.

Big hard kicks.

'Hey,' yells Uncle Cliff. 'That's not on.'

I try to be a positive manager.

'I think Matt's OK,' I say to Uncle Cliff. 'He's so fast and clever, Ayo's missing him most of the time.'

But not all the time. I can see Matt wincing when Ayo's boot hits him.

Sometimes, when you're an Aussie manager, you just have to have faith in Aussie leg pins.

'Looking good, Matt,' I yell.

'Don't worry,' says a man standing next to us. 'The boys will be fine.'

The man looks like he could be Ayo's dad.

'Where I come from,' says Uncle Cliff to the man, 'people go to jail for hurting each other like that. Unless they're at the Boxing Day sales.'

'It's normal,' says the man. 'Trust me. I know. I've got boys training with six clubs.'

I stare at him. If he's Ayo's dad, he must have a very talented family.

'Rupert Nkrumo,' says the man, holding out his

hand to Uncle Cliff. 'All Africa Sports And Talent Agency.'

Uncle Cliff goes to shake Mr Nkrumo's hand, then sees what Matt and Ayo are doing.

Ayo's got the ball, and Matt is trying to tackle him. Ayo is using his elbows to make it hard for Matt to concentrate. It must be very hard to concentrate when your kidneys are being bashed.

'Stop that, you two,' yells Uncle Cliff, hurrying onto the pitch.

Mr Nkrumo is still holding his hand out.

I shake it.

'Pleased to meet you,' I say.

'That man is your father?' says Mr Nkrumo, pointing to Uncle Cliff, who's being yelled at by one of the trainers.

'Uncle,' I say. 'But he takes the job very seriously.'

Mr Nkrumo nods.

'Of course,' he says. 'Every job should be taken seriously. The world is a serious place. Plenty of time to relax when you're dead.'

I look at him, puzzled. Why does everybody here always talk about dying?

'Harder,' shouts Mr Nkrumo.

I'm shocked. He's shouting it to Ayo, who's bashing into Matt with both shoulders.

'Excuse me,' I say sternly to Mr Nkrumo.

I'm about to let him know I take my job of looking after Matt seriously, but before I can, Uncle Cliff comes back with a dejected face.

'I've been sent off,' he says.

I know how hurtful that must be for an ex-referee. I hold Uncle Cliff's hand.

'Thanks,' he says. 'But they told me I have to wait in the car park.'

He heads off.

'Foolish man,' says Mr Nkrumo. 'Family and agents are not allowed on the pitch. I could have told him that.'

I'm starting to not like Mr Nkrumo very much. I've read about soccer agents like him. They might be good at getting players an extra ten thousand a week and a better parking spot, but they're not very warm-hearted.

Oh no, now Matt and Ayo are chest to chest with the ball on the ground between them, trying to knock each other over just using their hips.

Can't the trainers do something?

At last, Mr Merchant the head coach is calling Ayo and Matt over.

He should have done this ten minutes ago. Cooled them down. Told them this sort of behaviour isn't acceptable.

'I've been watching you two,' says Mr Merchant. 'In the old days you'd both have been sent off for doing that. And suspended for a month.'

Matt's face falls.

'But this isn't the old days,' says Mr Merchant. 'So let's see what positives we can take out of this. Good aggression. Good application. Exactly what a first team player needs. Just don't let the ref see.'

He slaps them both on the back.

Ayo grins. Matt looks a bit stunned.

So am I.

Training finishes with the boys splitting into two teams and having a match. Which is a relief. A match will give Matt a much better chance to show his skill.

And he does.

He scores two brilliant goals, both times using balance and speed to avoid some very rough tackles. And when he gets turned and held and bashed into, he just jumps up and gets back into the game.

'Good on you, Matt,' I yell.

I'm proud of him. He's learning to cope with soccer at the highest level.

Mostly. But there is one part of it he's not coping with so well.

Each time Matt scores, not one of his team looks happy or says well done. Even when he tries to set up goals for them, the boys in his team don't give him a single friendly look.

I remind myself why this is happening. It's because they all want to be the one. When somebody else sets up a goal for them, they worry that the other person is being the one.

Once Matt is out of all this and in the first team, things'll be better. I must remind him of that.

Matt's not reminding himself. He's starting to look dejected. Just little signs only a sister can spot.

Trying to hide a sigh by picking his nose. Shoulders drooping when he scratches his private parts.

'Team Sutherland,' I yell, because I think that's what Uncle Cliff would do if he was here.

At the end of training I give Matt a high-five and tell him how brilliant he was.

'A lot of positives we can take out of today,' I say.

That seems to cheer him up a bit.

'Where's Uncle Cliff?' he says.

'Got sent off,' I say.

Matt grins, which is good to see.

But as he heads off to get changed and I go to the car park to find Uncle Cliff, I start feeling a bit dejected myself.

Matt is so friendly and generous and kind, I just wish he didn't have to put up with all this unfriendliness. I wish there was some way I could make it easier for him.

I stop being dejected.

Managers don't get dejected, they get working.

I ask myself if there's any way of making this academy a happier and friendlier place.

21

Uncle Cliff is a champ. After breakfast, as soon as Matt leaves for training, I tell him what I think we should do and he swings into action.

First we rent a car.

Uncle Cliff tries to get a discount on the basis of me having asthma. The rental woman won't give us one, but adds an extra five free minutes to the rental period so I don't have to hurry to where the car is parked.

Which is very kind and friendly. Exactly the sort of thing we're planning to encourage at the academy.

Then we rent a barbecue. The party supply rental person doesn't give discounts either. Neither does the butcher (sausages) or the supermarket manager (onions, rolls and fizzy drinks).

It doesn't matter. They say no in a friendly way. And at least we get the sausage sizzle set up in time.

'Come on, lads,' calls Uncle Cliff from the academy car park as the under-fifteens troop off the training pitch. 'Have a sausage and a drink, then we'll have a kick-around, just for fun.'

The boys all look at him blankly.

So do their parents.

I can feel my insides going sausage-shaped. This felt like such a good idea. An Aussie-style barbie and kick-around. To remind the academy boys how much better football is when it's fun. And to get everyone relaxed so Matt can make some friends.

But not one kid picks up a sausage.

Well, one.

'Put it back,' says his mother. 'It's not on the club diet. I've got your protein powder waiting at home.'

The boy puts the sausage back and gets into a car with his mother.

I see Ayo heading towards a minibus with Mr Nkrumo.

'Ayo,' I yell. 'Come and have a sausage.'

Mr Nkrumo says something to Ayo, who looks across at us, gives us an apologetic shrug and gets into the minibus.

A cold grey wind springs up and blows away the yummy sausage and onion smells.

All the other boys and parents are getting into their cars.

Matt, who's been hanging back and looking embarrassed, comes over.

'G'day, Matty,' says Uncle Cliff. 'Hope you're

hungry. There's thirty-six sausages here for the three of us.'

'What are you doing?' says Matt. 'Most of these kids live miles away. Their parents spend hours driving them here. Nobody's got time to hang around for a dopey barbecue.'

I try not to feel hurt. And I hope Uncle Cliff doesn't either. We both know poor Matt's under a lot of pressure.

Matt's shoulders droop.

'Sorry,' he says, picking up a sausage. 'It's a good barbecue. I'm just a bit stressed and hyper cos I've been given a place in the under-fifteen team against Manchester United on Sunday.'

We both stare at him.

'Judas H brilliant,' I say, giving him a hug. 'Matt, you've done it.'

'Rock 'n' roll,' says Uncle Cliff, giving Matt a hug too. 'Team Sutherland.'

'That's it,' says a loud voice. 'Finish. Pack it up.'

A stern-looking person in a tracksuit is striding towards us across the car park. It's Mr Merchant the head coach.

'We're celebrating,' says Uncle Cliff. 'Have a sausage. Six if you like.'

Mr Merchant ignores the offer.

'Go and get changed, Matt,' he says.

Matt looks uncertain. Then he heads off to the changing room.

Mr Merchant gives the barbecue a sour look.

'When you've got this unauthorised facility packed away,' he says to Uncle Cliff, 'please regard yourself as banned from the academy grounds.'

We stare at him.

'So that's no to a sausage?' says Uncle Cliff.

'This club,' says Mr Merchant, 'has just made a significant gesture of faith in Matt. Foolish antics like this are not helping him.'

'Am I banned too?' I say.

Mr Merchant looks at me. He shakes his head.

'You're a child,' he says. 'You can't be expected to know any better.'

'This barbecue was my idea,' I say indignantly.

'Exactly,' says Mr Merchant, giving Uncle Cliff and me very stern looks, like he wants to put us off helping Matt for good.

He's wasting his time.

When your brother's playing his first match against Manchester United in three days, nothing puts you off.

As Mr Merchant strides away, somebody else calls my name.

I turn.

Ken is hurrying over from the office building.

'Bridie,' he says. 'I've had a special request from our Australian media friends. It's quite a cute idea and I think we can make it happen.'

He stops and stares at the barbecue.

I wait patiently. Grown-ups sometimes take a while to get to the point.

'Good barbecue,' says Ken. 'What a shame the media aren't here today.'

'Sausage?' says Uncle Cliff.

Ken takes one. Then he remembers he'd started to tell me something.

'This Saturday,' he says through a mouthful of sausage, 'our first team's playing Liverpool. On match days, when our team runs out into the stadium, we always have our mascots leading us. The Aussie media want one of the mascots on Saturday to be you.'

I'm a bit stunned.

I look at Uncle Cliff. I can see he thinks it's an exciting idea. After a few moments I start to feel that way too.

If I become a mascot, maybe I can help make this club a happier place for Matt.

But I'm a bit nervous as well.

The thought of going into a stadium in front of a huge crowd of people is giving me butterflies in my tummy.

Oh well, at least it's better than the sausage feeling I was having earlier.

22

I'm helping Mrs Jarvis make fishcakes.

'Try to take all the bones out,' she says. 'We don't want Uncle Cliff to get stabbed. Though that's probably happening right now if the diet experts at the academy have heard about his sausage exploits.'

I remind Mrs Jarvis that Uncle Cliff is banned and he has to wait by the gate, so he'll be safe.

Mrs Jarvis chuckles.

'A barbecue,' she says. 'What a harebrained scheme. That man, honestly.'

I open my mouth to tell her that the barbecue was my idea. All that comes out is a yawn. I was awake half the night worrying about being a mascot tomorrow. That's why I'm too tired to go to training today.

'Sorry,' I say. 'I'm finding it a bit hard to concentrate.'

Mrs Jarvis gives me a sympathetic smile.

'You'll be a fab mascot,' she says. 'And I've asked a friend over to give you a few tips. She was a mascot for three years.'

I stare at Mrs Jarvis. That is so kind.

'Thank you,' I say.

'Bones,' says Mrs Jarvis.

I concentrate on the fish until the front doorbell rings.

'I'll get it,' says Mrs Jarvis, wiping her hands.

She heads off down the hall. I wash my hands to get rid of the fishy smell and go after her.

I'm glad I used hot water and soap, because standing by the front door holding her hand out to me is the girlfriend of one of the most famous footballers in the world.

'Wotcha, Bridie,' says Terrine. 'Alright?'

'Yes,' I say, my voice a bit squeaky with surprise. 'Thanks.'

'Why don't you two go and sit by the fire,' says Mrs Jarvis. 'I'll make some tea.'

I follow Terrine into the lounge room and we sit down.

Terrine can probably see I'm still feeling a bit surprised, so she explains that she's known Mrs Jarvis for years, ever since Gazz was an academy boy staying here at the house.

'Is that how you met Gazz?' I say. 'Being a mascot?'

Terrine nods and starts to sob.

I'm not sure what to do. Managers don't have to deal with tears that often. Plus I'm a bit worried Terrine's going to tell me bad things about being a mascot.

After a few moments I go and sit next to her on the settee and pat her arm. It doesn't seem to do much good.

Mrs Jarvis comes in, puts her tray down and hurries over.

'Oh, love,' she says to Terrine. 'What's wrong?'

'It's Gazz,' sobs Terrine. 'He's just so unhappy.'

Mrs Jarvis sits on the other side of Terrine and pats her other arm.

'I'd offer you some fishcakes to take back for him,' says Mrs Jarvis. 'But I'm sensing this is a bit more serious than that.'

Terrine nods and sniffs.

'He's miserable nearly all the time,' she says, drying her tears. 'And he used to be so happy when he started out.'

Mrs Jarvis nods.

'I remember,' she says. 'A couple of years after he got in the first team, another club offered forty-three million for him. He was that chuffed.'

'The longer Gazz spends at the top,' says Terrine, 'the more anxious and miserable he gets. Specially when the club loses a few matches. You've seen Gazz's den, Mrs J. There's about eight screens in there. All the big clubs show their games online and Gazz watches them over and over. He's panicked the club's going to buy some younger player to replace him. He's in there for hours most days. It's like he's in prison.'

'Oh, love,' says Mrs Jarvis. 'It can't be that bad.'

'Even my brother's happier than Gazz,' says Terrine tearfully. 'And he's actually in prison.'

Mrs Jarvis murmurs sympathetically.

'Sometimes I wish none of this had ever happened,' says Terrine. 'The money, the house, the Scrabble nights with Shane Warne. Sometimes I wish Gazz was back playing football on the council estate where he grew up. He was happy then.'

Mrs Jarvis sighs again. This is the first time I've seen her not know what to say. We both do more patting.

I don't know what to say either.

All I can think of is Matt.

If his dream comes true, in a few years he could be like Gazz.

I can't let that happen. I can't just stand by while Matt becomes a fabulously successful international soccer star and ends up miserable.

I've got to do something.

23

'Where's Matt?' I say to Ken, which isn't easy with a mouthful of fake fur.

I thought Matt was coming here to the changing room where I'm putting on this mascot costume. So the Aussie media could interview us both together before the match starts.

'Change of plan,' says Ken. 'Matt and your Uncle Cliff and Mrs Jarvis are in a VIP box up in the stadium.'

Ken explains there's another film crew up there with them. The media people want to film Matt and Uncle Cliff's faces when they see me in this costume for the first time as I go out onto the pitch.

'They'll be pretty amazed,' says Ken.

I don't argue. I'm pretty amazed myself. I thought the mascot outfit would be the club shirt and shorts. Maybe with a sash. I had no idea that one of the world's most important football clubs would have mascots who are creatures made of brightly coloured fluffy fake fur.

'Looking good,' says Ken, smiling in through the eye-holes in my furry head.

I'm the baby mascot. The grown-up mascot, a woman called Trude who's been doing it for three years, gives me a thumbs up.

'Nervous?' asks the media interviewer.

'A bit,' I say. 'But I want to get good at being a mascot so I can do it when my brother Matt's playing in the team.'

The interviewer glances at Ken. She doesn't seem to know what to say next.

I want to ask her if there's ever been a manager in the Premier League who was also a mascot. But before I can get the fluff out of my mouth, Ken hurries me and Trude out of the changing room.

'Five-minute call,' he says, which must be a technical mascot term.

I don't know which kids have been in this suit before, but it smells strange in here. Sort of like old marmalade.

The players of both teams are lined up in a tunnel that leads out into the stadium. I can't believe it. I'm in a big tube with some of the most famous footballers in the world.

I can hear the distant sound of thousands of voices. Like roaring surf. Suddenly I'm feeling a bit panicky. I try to keep my breathing good.

Ken takes me and Trude to the front of the line.

Our players all pat me on the head. Gazz is one of them.

'Lookin' fit, Bridie,' he says, which is kind of him.

The Liverpool mascots are here too. I hold out my hand to shake, but they don't want to. Maybe there's a rule about mascots not being mates.

Loud music starts playing and Ken gives me a little push.

'Go,' he says.

I waddle out into the stadium, holding Trude's furry paw.

So far this trip, some pretty amazing things have happened, but nothing as Judas H amazing as walking out into a Premier League stadium for the first time.

As I step onto the grass, I notice that the air smells really fresh and damp. Just like at home when me and Dad go for an early morning walk before it gets hot. Except that when we walk into the cemetery at 6 a.m. there isn't an explosion of so much noise you want to push nylon fluff into your ears.

And there aren't more people than you've ever seen. Over forty thousand, that's what Ken said.

Now I'm starting to fully panic. It feels like they're all looking at me.

I'm starting to wheeze.

Maybe I should have told Ken about my medical condition. Maybe these mascot suits aren't so good for asthma. And I've left my puffer in the changing room.

To help me breathe, I pretend the stadium's full of everybody Dad has ever moved and all their families yelling and clapping and singing to show Dad how much they appreciate him not breaking any of their ornaments or squashing their pets.

That's better.

Ken said me and Trude have to walk around and wave to them all for a few minutes, which is what we're doing.

I try to see where Matt and Uncle Cliff and Mrs Jarvis are, but I can't.

It's like trying to spot three tiny figures in a huge roaring ocean. We went on holiday to Surfers once, and the only way you could see Uncle Cliff when he was in the sea was from his orange shower cap. He's not wearing a shower cap today.

I look harder but I still can't see Matt.

Suddenly I start to feel anxious again.

I tell myself not to be dopey. Brothers don't just disappear, not even in crowds this huge. Not when they've got uncles and landladies with them.

After a bit, Trude says something to me that I can't hear because of the humungous noise. She leads me to some seats right at the edge of the pitch.

Ken sits down next to me and puts his face close to my furry head.

'We'll watch the match from here,' he shouts. 'So you can go back on the pitch at half-time.'

I nod. I have to remember I'm doing a job. A serious job.

The match starts.

The players all know they're doing a serious job too. You can tell by the way they hurl themselves at each other. Soccer doesn't look this serious when you watch it on telly. On TV you can't hear the players grunting and swearing and the sound of their bodies crunching into each other.

Now, when they come close to my seat, I can hear it even over the angry yelling noise of the crowd.

Gazz gets the ball and dribbles towards the Liverpool goal. He does a really skilful move round one player, but two more go for him. One grabs his shirt and the other barges him over.

'Hey,' I yell, jumping up. 'That's cheating.'

I don't think the referee hears me, partly because most of the fans are yelling at him too and also because my furry mascot head doesn't have a very big mouth-hole.

A few minutes later, Gazz barges a Liverpool player over.

This time the ref sees it and has a word with Gazz. I wish I could hear what the ref is saying. 'Come on, play nicely,' is what I'd say. 'Where's the fun in hurting each other?'

If I was the ref I'd also have a word to the crowd. Tell them to shout friendlier things. Of course players are going to get overexcited with about forty thousand grumpy people urging them on.

But the ref doesn't do any of that.

I glance at Ken and Trude. They don't seem

bothered at all by what's going on. Until somebody in the crowd throws something. It hits Trude on her furry head and splatters her and Ken. It's a half-eaten hamburger with lots of tomato sauce. Luckily most of it misses me, but I'm still shocked.

'Are you OK?' I say.

Ken nods and takes Trude off to get cleaned up.

On the pitch things aren't much better. Players pushing and pulling each other and holding and barging and turning and bashing into each other. The ref sees most of it but he doesn't seem to care. He only blows his whistle if players trip each other or tread on each other's feet. It's like he's more interested in protecting their expensive boots.

I watch the players' faces. This is something else you don't see on TV. How anxious and stressed they all are, not just Gazz. They might be stars who need special wallets, but none of them look like they're enjoying themselves one bit.

Slowly my heart sinks and my fake fur droops.

If Matt's dream comes true, this will be his life. Year after year of violence and unfriendliness. And sooner or later, he'll turn into a violent and unfriendly person himself.

I've seen it starting already at training.

I stare at the players.

All famous. All rich. All the one.

What went wrong?

Is it just habit? After years of playing this way, have they just forgotten how to have fun?

Maybe they just need somebody to remind them.

Urgently.

Here and now.

I look around the pitch. The ref isn't reminding them. The managers aren't reminding them. The crowd isn't reminding them.

It'll have to be me.

24

I'm keeping an eye on the stadium clock.

That way I'll know when the referee is about to blow his whistle for half-time. So I can get back on the pitch without wasting a second and have a word with him.

I'll remind him how much fun soccer used to be when he was a kid. And when all the players were kids as well. And how grateful everyone would be if he could ask them to play like that again.

And send them off if they don't.

I think it's better if I say it to the referee and get him to say it to the players. They'll probably listen to him more than they'll listen to a fluffy baby creature doing muffled wheezing.

Thirty seconds to go.

Except the referee doesn't actually blow his whistle for another fifty seconds.

I don't blame him. If I had to spend forty-five

minutes running around a pitch with such a miserable bunch of players, I'd probably get slightly depressed and forget the time as well.

As soon as the ref blows the whistle, I jump up and waddle towards him as fast as I can. Which isn't very fast because this furry head is a bit big and the eye-holes are in slightly different places to my eyes. Plus I have to remember to wave to the crowd and I'm a bit short of breath.

I lose sight of the ref for a while, but when I adjust my head I see him again.

He's staring at me and talking into the small microphone he's got clipped to his face. He's probably telling the person who makes his half-time cuppa to hold off for a couple of minutes because a mascot wants a word with him.

All the players are staring at me as well.

This is good. If they were all heading straight off for their cuppas, they wouldn't be able to hear what the ref is about to tell them.

'Excuse me,' I say to the ref, using my biggest voice because of the muffling.

This is hopeless. He can't hear me.

I take my head off.

'Excuse me,' I say. 'Remember when you were a kid? I bet when you were on a soccer pitch you didn't stop giggling half the time.'

The referee's mouth is open, like he's completely forgotten all about that.

Or is he just angry?

Then I see what Gazz is doing near the ref. He's placing the ball carefully on the pitch as if he's about to take a free kick.

I look at him.

He looks at me.

'Get off,' roars the referee, waving his arm angrily at me.

I realise what's happened.

Judas H.

I'm in the middle of the pitch. In the middle of a Premier League match. Forty thousand people are looking at me. And millions on TV.

Except it's not the middle of the match.

Not quite.

I forgot that at the end of each half of a professional football match there's an extra bit added on. It's called injury time. Three or four minutes of extra play, which the teams are waiting to get on with now.

'Off,' roars the referee at me.

We don't need injury time when we play on our waste ground at home because none of us have ever been injured.

In my case, that might all be about to change.

Angry security guards are sprinting towards me.

I try to run.

I'm struggling for breath.

Suddenly I'm feeling more anxious than all the soccer stars on the pitch put together.

I'm wheezing worse than I have for ages.

I lie down on the grass. The stadium is still very loud, but the noise sounds like we're all under water.

Something is squeezing my chest very tight. Really, really tight. It's not my furry costume, and it's not bubble wrap.

'Matt,' I try to yell, but I can't.

25

The managers of big famous football clubs always have big impressive offices. Jean-Pierre Michel's is very big and very impressive.

This would probably take some people's breath away, being here. But I've only just got my breathing back, and I'm trying not to lose it again.

I decide Jean-Pierre Michel probably uses the inner part of his office for private stuff, and the outer part for yelling at mascots who disrupt Premier League matches.

So I'm a bit surprised when Ken takes me into the inner part.

Which is empty.

'He'll be here soon,' mutters Ken, looking unhappy and a little bit sauce-splattered.

'Are you in trouble too?' I ask.

Ken doesn't reply.

I can see this whole experience has been

very stressful for him. He was stressed when the ambulance officers carried me off the pitch and gave me oxygen. He was stressed after I got changed out of the fluffy suit and he took it away from me and locked it in a cupboard. And he was stressed at the end of the game when he came to the VIP box where I watched the second half with Matt and Uncle Cliff and Mrs Jarvis. At first I thought Ken's last bit of stress was because we'd just lost two–nil, but then he told me the manager wanted to see me.

I think Jean-Pierre Michel is a French name. Several of the Premier League managers are French. I think they like working in England because the fish and chips are so good.

I can hear Jean-Pierre Michel talking in the outer office where Uncle Cliff and Matt are waiting. And I can hear Uncle Cliff standing up for me in a loud voice.

'She's a kid,' he's saying. 'All kids are idiots sometimes.'

He means well.

Jean-Pierre Michel comes in. He's quite a big man and he's wearing a suit that's really well ironed. But he looks even more tired than Mum and Dad. And now he's here, Ken looks even more stressed.

'Guv,' says Ken. 'It's my fault. The Australian media –'

Jean-Pierre Michel puts his finger to his lips.

Ken stops talking.

'So,' says Jean-Pierre Michel, looking at me. 'We spend millions of pounds to keep hooligans out of our stadium, and then our mascot turns out to be a hooligan.'

'That's not fair, Guv,' says Ken.

He's right, it's not.

'Excuse me, Mr Michel,' I say. 'I'm not a hooligan. I just think soccer should be fun.'

Jean-Pierre Michel looks like he has a tummy pain.

'Fun?' he says.

'Yes,' I say. 'Fun.'

Jean-Pierre Michel shakes his head wearily. I think he wants us to go.

'Thank you, Ken,' he says. 'I just wanted to see your mascot choice for myself.'

Ken looks like he has a huge tummy pain. And it's my fault.

'All those goals your players missed today,' I say to Jean-Pierre Michel. 'People can't do their best shots when they're feeling miserable and possibly concussed, it's a known fact.'

I'm not sure if Mr Michel hears me. He's looking at stuff on his desk.

Ken hears me.

'Come on,' he says anxiously. 'Time to go.'

He tries to push me out of the office.

I do something I've seen Matt do a lot. I drop my shoulders and roll my hips and slide away from Ken.

'My friend Gael-Anne,' I say to Mr Michel, 'she used to hate soccer at school. Then she started having fun with us on the waste ground and now she can do headers and everything.'

'Bridie,' hisses Ken. 'That's enough.'

He grabs my shoulders and pulls me towards the door.

Jean-Pierre Michel is standing at his desk with his back to me and it doesn't look like he's heard a word.

That's what I think at first.

But just as Ken is dragging me out the door, Jean-Pierre Michel turns and gives me a stare.

For a second I think he's going to agree with me.

Then his face changes and I can see he isn't.

I wish I could believe you, his face says. But I'm one of the most respected and experienced and highly paid football managers in the world, and you're just a kid with nylon fluff in her hair.

26

When Mum and Dad see me being a mascot on YouTube, Mum gets upset and Skypes.

She says that from now on I have to stay indoors with Mrs Jarvis.

'No,' I say. 'Please don't make me. I'm fine.'

'You didn't look fine on that stretcher,' says Mum, getting more upset.

Poor Mum. It's a big jump, going from me living at home helping with the washing-up to the neighbours telling her at six in the morning I've been carried off a UK Premier League soccer pitch by two ambulance officers and several security guards.

Uncle Cliff explains to Mum that ambulance officers always put people on stretchers, it's their training, even at rock concerts.

'The more people they carry off,' says Matt, 'the more they get paid.'

It's good of Matt and Uncle Cliff to try and help Mum feel better.

'You're still grounded,' Mum says to me.

Dad nods sternly.

'I can't be,' I plead. 'Matt needs me at his match tomorrow. It's his bit chance.'

Dad sighs.

'You're grounded, love,' he says. 'Don't fight it.'

But I have to.

'I'm Matt's manager,' I say tearfully. 'I have to look after him. You don't know how rough and dangerous it is over here.'

As soon as I say it I know I shouldn't have.

Matt and Uncle Cliff are glaring at me.

'Bridie's being a bit dramatic,' says Uncle Cliff hurriedly to Mum and Dad. 'It's only a little bit rough and dangerous. Hardly ever. Matt'll be fine. His leg pins are doing brilliantly.'

Mum and Dad glance at each other. They look unhappy.

'Matt, love,' says Mum. 'There's something we have to tell you. We should have told you before, but . . . well, at the time we thought it was for the best.'

She hesitates and glances at Dad again.

I can see they feel bad about saying it, whatever it is.

'What?' says Matt.

We're all getting very tense at this end.

'Remember what I told you after the accident,'

says Mum. 'How the doctors in the hospital said your legs were fragile because of the pins? Well that wasn't true, love. I made it up.'

We all stare at her.

'Actually,' says Dad, looking ashamed, 'the pins make your legs stronger.'

'I'm sorry, love,' says Mum. 'I should have told you the truth. But I was just desperate for you to look after yourself and not get hurt any more.'

We all take this in.

Matt specially.

'We are sorry, Matt,' says Dad.

Matt thinks about it for a bit longer.

'It's OK,' he says. 'I don't blame you. But thanks for telling me.'

'Hope it helps in your match tomorrow,' says Mum quietly.

'We're proud of you, son,' says Dad.

'Thanks,' says Matt.

Dad puts his arm round Mum and she takes a deep breath as if she's relieved that's over.

Mrs Jarvis comes in and Mum explains to her that I'm grounded. Mrs Jarvis gives me a sympathetic look.

'Oh dear,' she says to Mum and Dad. 'That's a little bit tricky tomorrow because I'm going to the match too. It's a very important one.'

'Manchester United,' says Uncle Cliff. 'They're coming all the way from Manchester.'

Mum and Dad hesitate.

I can see they're not sure what to say.

'What if I promise to keep an eye on Bridie,' says Mrs Jarvis, 'and make sure she's completely fine.'

Mum and Dad look at each other.

'Alright,' says Mum. 'Seeing as it's Manchester United.'

Dad gives us a thumbs up.

After we all say goodbye and click Skype off, Uncle Cliff punches the air.

'Rock 'n' roll,' he says to Matt. 'Aussie leg pins.'

Matt looks delighted too. He gives Uncle Cliff and me and Mrs Jarvis high-fives.

I'm relieved but I'm not delighted. Because I know why Matt's so happy. Now he doesn't have to hold back. Now he can throw himself totally into going for his dream and impressing the academy trainers and coaches.

Now he can be as violent and unfriendly as he wants.

27

*I*n the car on the way to the Manchester United match, I suddenly remember that Uncle Cliff is still banned.

'It's not fair,' I say. 'An uncle shouldn't miss a match like this just because of a sausage sizzle.'

In the front, Mrs Jarvis and Uncle Cliff swap a smile.

'No need for concern love,' says Mrs Jarvis to me.

'I'll be right, Bridie,' says Uncle Cliff. 'I've got my guardian angel with me. She knows important people in high places. By their first names.'

Hearing me mention the sausage sizzle has made Mrs Jarvis amused all over again.

'Club nutritionists would have had kittens,' she chuckles. 'Low-fat kittens, but kittens.'

'They were gourmet sausages,' says Uncle Cliff indignantly. 'Pork and peanut.'

'Not a good idea, Cliff,' says Mrs Jarvis. 'If one

of the lads was allergic he'd go into anaphylactic shock and his lungs would seize up.'

Uncle Cliff gives Mrs Jarvis an adoring look. Then he glances at Matt.

'How you feeling, Matty?' he says. 'Ready for your big chance?'

I glance over at Matt. He nods. He doesn't look too nervous, which is good.

'I had a big chance once,' says Uncle Cliff. 'It was the open-mike number at a Stones tribute gig. I could have joined the back-up singers on "You Can't Always Get What You Want". Paula would have been majorly impressed. But I chickened out and she gave her Skype log-in details to the lead singer.'

We all stay quiet for a bit.

'Don't torture yourself, Cliff,' says Mrs Jarvis after a while. 'It probably would have happened anyway.'

We stay quiet for a bit more.

'I'm not going to chicken out,' says Matt suddenly. 'So you don't have to worry.'

'We know you won't, Matt,' says Mrs Jarvis.

'You'll be brilliant,' I say.

I don't say brilliant at what. I'm hoping it'll be skill.

When we arrive, Mrs Jarvis jumps out and chats with the security guard at the gate.

They look like they know each other.

'Sorted,' says Mrs Jarvis to Uncle Cliff when she

gets back into the car. 'I explained to Brian I'll have a word with Neal Merchant about your ban.'

'You're amazing,' says Uncle Cliff.

After we park, Mrs Jarvis walks straight over to Mr Merchant at the edge of the under-fifteen pitch. By the time me and Uncle Cliff get there, she's still talking and he's not getting a word in. But he doesn't look cross. Probably because the Aussie media are filming us all.

'I'll let you go now, Neal,' Mrs Jarvis is saying. 'I'm sure you want to have a word to the ref about keeping a lid on things today.'

I know what she means. Not letting the players get too violent.

'Thanks, Stella,' says Mr Merchant with a thin smile. 'You might want to have a word to certain members of your party about keeping a lid on things too.'

He looks at me and Uncle Cliff.

I know what he means. Us not running onto the pitch or having illegal barbecues.

'Always nice to talk, Neal,' says Mrs Jarvis sweetly.

Mr Merchant nods and walks off.

'He's lucky I didn't give him a Liverpool lump,' says Uncle Cliff, flexing his neck muscles.

'I think you mean a Liverpool kiss, Cliff,' says Mrs Jarvis. 'A Liverpool lump is a cake.'

'Is Uncle Cliff unbanned?' I ask.

'Sorted,' says Mrs Jarvis.

Uncle Cliff gazes at her. I think he's in love.

The teams come out, Manchester United first. They look pretty tough. And big. More like under-sixteen than under-fifteen. A bit like the orange team back home, except smarter and much more talented and no dog bites.

Then Matt comes out with his team. I'm so thrilled and proud to see Matt wearing the shirt of such a famous club. But I'm also feeling a bit nervous in the tummy about what Manchester United will do to him once they see how good he is. And what he'll do back to them.

I give Matt a little wave, so he can see how proud I am. He sees me and waves back.

'Go, Matty,' yells Uncle Cliff.

'Use your skill,' says Mrs Jarvis quietly.

She smiles at me and I smile back.

But Matt doesn't use much of his skill at first. At first he just does some careful tackling and passing, and puts up with being held and turned and bashed into. I think he feels a bit nervous about playing against such a legendary team.

Then, about twenty minutes in, he starts being mesmerising. At first it's mostly to protect himself, gliding and dancing the ball past the roughest Man U defenders, his feet going like those casters on fridges that can go in any direction.

For a bit the Manchester United players have trouble grasping the idea that somebody is getting past them so often. But then they do and they start going for Matt big time.

They can't touch him. He's just too fast and skilful.

'Good boy,' says Mrs Jarvis.

'Dance like a butterfly, sting like a bee,' yells Uncle Cliff.

I think that must be a Rolling Stones song.

At first Matt doesn't score himself. He sets up chances for other people, specially Ayo. They're good chances, but Man U are very good defenders and none of the chances come off.

When Matt says bad luck to his team-mates, they don't even look at him. Except Ayo, who gives him a tiny nod sometimes.

Then Manchester United score. A good build-up with some very fast passing, a long through-ball and a superb finish.

This changes things for Matt, I can tell from the shape of his shoulders.

A few minutes later, he beats two players on the edge of their penalty area and sees the rest of the Man U defenders moving into position, which is what a class side will always do. Matt turns away from them and for a while he's dribbling towards his own goal. Until he turns again and shoots all in one movement. The ball blurs over everybody's heads and dips into the top corner of the goal before their goalie can move.

People just stare at him.

Our players, their players, our trainers, their trainers, our family members, their family members. Even the big black birds in the bare trees look stunned.

At half-time, as Matt trots off towards the changing rooms, I wave and he gives me a little one back.

He doesn't look very happy.

I don't understand. Matt is playing brilliantly. He's scored and he's using his skill to avoid bruises. Why isn't he pleased?

'He doesn't look very happy,' says Uncle Cliff. 'Is he pooing regularly?'

I think it probably isn't that, but I don't know what it is.

Then in the second half I do.

For the first fifteen minutes after the break, Matt goes back to setting up chances for the others. And this time he makes them even better chances. Ayo scores. So does another of our boys.

Three–one to us.

After both the goals Matt goes to congratulate the scorer. Both times they ignore him, even Ayo.

It's exactly the same problem. We've talked about it after training matches, me and Matt, and he says he understands how everyone's anxious about being the one. But now it's happening again, he looks even more unhappy.

I can see him losing interest in the match. He hardly touches the ball for ages.

'Matt,' yells Uncle Cliff, waving his arms. 'Come on. What's wrong?'

'He looks like a very disappointed young man to me,' says Mrs Jarvis quietly.

I agree with her.

'Well he doesn't have to be,' says Uncle Cliff. 'If he's disappointed in himself he can do something about it.'

'I don't think he's disappointed in himself, Cliff,' says Mrs Jarvis. 'I think he's disappointed with what's happened to top-level professional football in the first part of the twenty-first century.'

Uncle Cliff thinks about this.

'Matt,' he yells. 'Come on. Don't let top-level professional football in the first part of the twenty-first century get you down.'

I don't know if Matt hears this, or if it's something else that sparks him, like the elbow in the head he gets from one of his own team as they're jumping for a high cross.

But suddenly Matt is on fire.

Not in a good way.

A Manchester United midfielder is dribbling and Matt runs at him and tackles him.

Hard.

The boy drops like a mattress, and Matt goes sprawling. But it's legal because Matt played the ball not the man. Legal, but Mum would be horrified. Matt and the Man U player are both looking dazed as they get up. I can hear Uncle Cliff's leather jacket creaking with tension. I'm glad he wasn't videoing that bit on his phone.

'Go easy,' mutters Uncle Cliff.

I agree. We both have faith in Aussie leg pins, but there are plenty of other parts of Matt that can get hurt.

Matt doesn't go easy. He throws himself into tackles again and again. He's like a wallaby bouncing off a herd of elephants.

Then another high cross comes in and lots of the boys jump for it. Except half of them can't get off the ground because the other half are holding them.

Including Matt.

I can't believe it. He's got two big fistfuls of another boy's shirt.

Soon after, he turns somebody, jabbing his knee behind theirs so they drop to the ground.

I feel a bit sick.

But not as sick as I do a few minutes later when Matt goes sprawling after missing a big tackle.

The Manchester United boy holds out a hand to help him up.

Matt knocks it away.

His angry face makes me want to cry. Mrs Jarvis looks pretty upset too. Uncle Cliff looks bewildered.

'Why's he playing like this?' says Uncle Cliff. 'Maybe he's homesick. Have there been any signs? Has he been calling out the names of Australian TV shows in his sleep?'

I shake my head.

But in a way, I realise, Uncle Cliff is right.

It's not Aussie TV Matt's missing. It's something even more important. The thing he had every day on our patch of waste ground at home. The thing he doesn't have here, not even when we're winning three–one.

The thing that makes soccer worth playing.

After the match the trainers and coaches are delighted, and Matt's the player they make the most fuss of. I don't think it's just because we won. I think they like the way he played.

When Matt comes over to us, he's got a big grin.

'They want me to play in the next match,' he says. 'They want us to stay longer in England. At least another week.'

For a moment I don't know what to say.

Then I throw my arms round Matt to share his joyfulness.

So does Mrs Jarvis.

I hug Uncle Cliff as well.

'Rock 'n' roll,' says Uncle Cliff. 'I'm over the moon about this.'

'Actually, Cliff,' says Mrs Jarvis, 'if you were over the moon, the atmospheric vacuum would make your brains come out your ears.'

But she lets him hug her as well.

Uncle Cliff is right. This is the moment when Matt's family should rejoice with him.

But I can't get rid of a feeling deep in my guts. Something heavy and not-good. An out-of-control cattle truck type feeling.

I take a big breath and try to ignore it.

But I can't.

Because I know the awful truth.

If Matt keeps playing like this and makes it through to the first team, it won't be his legs that are permanently damaged by top-level professional football in the first part of the twenty-first century.

It'll be his gentle loving heart.

Half-time

28

I t's the middle of the night when I creep into Matt's room.

I don't knock.

This is too important and too urgent.

Matt is curled up in bed. The pale light from the street lamp is coming in through the curtains. It makes him look dead.

The door squeaks.

Matt opens his eyes and peers at me, blinking.

'You alright?' he says.

'I've been thinking,' I say.

He pats the bed. I don't sit down. Some things you say better when you're standing up.

'We have to go home, Matt,' I say. 'Before it's too late.'

Matt sits up, staring at me sleepily.

'Before what's too late?' he says.

'Everything,' I say. 'All this.'

'What are you talking about?' he says.

'Top-level professional football in the first part of the twenty-first century,' I say. 'What it's doing to you. It's turning you into somebody else.'

Matt doesn't say anything.

For a few moments I think he's going to agree with me.

I'm wrong.

'It's not doing anything to me,' he says. 'Few bruises, that's all. No problem, I've got reinforced legs, remember? Anyway, what was it Uncle Cliff said that time he hurt his back trying to walk like Mick Jagger? No pain, no gain.'

'Let's go home, Matt,' I say. 'Just come home and be with me and Mum and Dad.'

'That's stupid, Bridie,' he says. 'I'm doing this for them. And you. For all of us.'

'Do you want to end up like Gazz?' I say.

Matt frowns.

Before I can tell him all the reasons I don't want him to end up like Gazz, he jumps out of bed and glares at me.

'Yes, I do,' he says. 'Gazz's parents live in a six-bedroom circular house with a fabulous view of the Essex marshes. Ken told me.'

Matt doesn't get it.

'Gazz is really unhappy,' I say. 'Even unhappier than he would be if he was in prison with Terrine's brother.'

Matt looks puzzled.

That didn't come out right.

'Listen, Bridie,' says Matt. 'If you're homesick and you want to go home, that's OK. We'll tell Uncle Cliff. He'll take you.'

I stare at him, shocked.

'No way,' I say. 'My place is with you.'

'I'll be fine,' says Matt. 'But I think you'll be better off at home.'

'I'm not leaving you,' I say. 'I'm your manager.'

Matt gives me a sad smile. Then his face goes serious and determined again.

'Not any more,' he says quietly. 'You're fired.'

Second Half

Second half

29

'Mrs Jarvis,' I say, as soon as Matt and Uncle Cliff have left for training. 'Is there somewhere near here to have a fun kick-around?'

Mrs Jarvis wipes her hands on a tea towel and looks at me.

'A fun kick-around?' she says. 'Those boys at the academy wouldn't know a fun kick-around if it was going on in their own undies. For most of those lads, football has been the deadly serious centre of their universe since they were four.'

'I don't mean at the academy,' I say. 'I mean somewhere else. A council estate, say.'

Mrs Jarvis looks at me thoughtfully.

'I hope Matt knows how lucky he is to have you as his manager,' she says.

'I'm not his manager any more,' I say. 'Just his sister.'

Mrs Jarvis nods slowly.

I wish she'd answer my question. I'm feeling so guilty about what I'm planning to do I just want to get on and do it. Mum and Dad are really excited and proud about what's happening to Matt, and I hate spoiling it for them.

But I have to.

'You're not going to give up, are you?' says Mrs Jarvis. 'You're not going to rest until you find football being played as football should be played, so Matt can rediscover the joyful spirit of the beautiful game.'

I look at her.

'And then when he remembers what he's lost,' says Mrs Jarvis, 'maybe he'll have another think about whether he wants to be here.'

She's incredible. I haven't said anything about this. Perhaps the younger sisters of other academy trainees have tried to save their brothers' gentle loving hearts too.

'You're right,' I say. 'I'm not giving up, and all the rest of what you just said.'

'In which case,' says Mrs Jarvis, reaching for her coat, 'I'd better show you where the council estate is.'

30

The council estate isn't far.

As me and Mrs Jarvis walk into it, I look around, a bit fascinated.

I've never seen anywhere like it. There are heaps and heaps of houses, all the same and all with sort of grey pebbles stuck to them.

In the middle of the houses is a patch of waste ground almost exactly the same size as our pitch at home.

Perfect.

'I'll leave you here while I do some shopping,' says Mrs Jarvis.

I stare at her, surprised.

'You'll be better off exploring on your own,' she says. 'Sometimes grown-ups get in the way.'

I nod gratefully. I really hope Mum gets to meet Mrs Jarvis one day. You can learn really important things from wise landladies.

'Have fun,' says Mrs Jarvis, tucking my scarf into my ski parka and giving me a smile.

She heads off.

The waste ground is deserted. The local kids must still be in school.

Doesn't matter. I can see a lot of soccer is played here because there are two goals made from old plastic buckets and most of the grass is gone.

I walk slowly towards the middle of the pitch, imagining all the fun that happens here. And, even better, imagining Matt in the thick of it.

'Who are you?' growls a voice.

I turn round, startled.

Glaring at me is a girl with tangled blonde hair and pimples and a jacket that says Detroit Wrecking Crew. And a very big handbag. She looks a bit like one of the apprentice hairdressers at Curl Up And Dye in our main street. But younger and much tougher.

I tell her who I am. Not the ex-manager part, just my name.

'Why aren't you at school?' she says, stepping closer. Which makes her look even tougher and scarier.

I explain that where I come from, we're still on school holidays.

'What?' she says, staring at my tartan skirt. 'Scotland?'

'Australia,' I say.

I try to be friendly. And brave. If I can get out

142

of this without being bashed up, it'll be a good example for Mum and Dad of how they don't have to be so anxious about me because I can look after myself.

'Why aren't you at school?' I ask the girl in a friendly way.

She scowls.

'School is a fascist repressive regime with no respect for human dignity,' she says. 'Or body piercing.'

I nod. I've heard some schools are like that.

'I'm visiting England with my brother,' I say. 'He's looking for a kick-around. Can I bring him here?'

The girl thinks about this.

I don't tell her I'm hoping Matt will have so much fun here he'll remember what soccer should be like and forget about big wallets and chandeliers in the bathroom and come home with me. I don't want to put her off. It's a big responsibility, helping to save a complete stranger's gentle heart.

Plus this whole thing's a risk anyway if the other kids are as tough as her. But as Dad said once when he moved a dog kennel with the dog still in it, what's life without a risk or two? Though that was before.

'Is your brother good-looking?' says the girl.

I think for a moment. He could be, but he's my brother, so I don't really know.

'Yes,' I say. 'Probably.'

The girl laughs and her whole face changes.

It's like Mum says. Half the time what's on the outside doesn't tell you what's on the inside. For example at work she makes leather iPad holders that look like books.

'Massive,' says the girl. 'Drag him along.'

I ask her if Matt should bring a ball, and she makes a joke that in my opinion is more suited to the Horns And Tail Hotel. But she's Matt's age, so that's probably normal. I don't mind anyway because she's friendly now and she tells me her name is Lola.

Lola warns me that people have to be careful playing soccer here because years ago a whole lot of stolen car parts were buried in this waste ground and sometimes they poke up through the dirt. I tell her we're used to being careful because at home we have wombats.

She laughs again.

I'm starting to like her. She's tough and kind, which is what I hope to be one day.

Lola opens her handbag and takes out a soccer ball.

'Go in goal,' she says.

I explain I don't play, and why.

'Asthma doesn't stop you being a goalie,' she says, rolling her eyes. 'Anyway, it'll get better as soon as you give up smoking.'

I have a go in goal.

I'm a bit nervous, but I soon get the hang of it. Lola does gentle kicks at first, then undoes the zip on her jeans so she can do harder ones.

It's heaps of fun. And it turns out I'm quite good at saves. Probably because I've had so much experience trying to save Matt.

By the time me and Lola say goodbye, I'm really looking forward to Matt meeting her.

She's exactly what I need to help me get him back to Australia.

31

'**F**ar out,' says Uncle Cliff when I tell him about Lola and the council estate kick-around. 'Wait till Matt hears about this.'

'Let's not tell him,' I say. 'Let's make it a surprise. On our way to training tonight.'

Today is one of the days the under-fifteens go to their normal schools, so there's an extra training session later. Matt's come home for an afternoon break. He's upstairs with Uncle Cliff's computer. I think he's checking the prices of indoor waterfalls.

I hope I'm right about the surprise. I hope Matt will enjoy it more that way.

At first everything goes well. Matt is in the back of the car with me, reading a soccer strategy book he borrowed from Mrs Jarvis, so he doesn't even notice we're going to training a different way.

As we get close to the waste ground, we start to hear a sound that makes me tingle with excitement.

Kids having fun playing soccer.

Uncle Cliff and Mrs Jarvis give each other a smile.

The sound is making me feel a bit homesick, but that doesn't matter. The timing is perfect. Matt looks up from his book just as we turn a corner, and there they are, about ten kids passing and tackling and shooting with big grins on their faces.

Matt stares.

I'm pleased to see Lola is playing. And by the looks of it, she's not bad. Though she'd probably be even better if she put her handbag down.

'Fancy a kick-around?' says Uncle Cliff to Matt. 'We've got time.'

Matt doesn't have to say anything. I can see from his face the answer is Judas H yes.

Then his face changes.

'Nah,' he says quietly. 'It's OK.'

He goes back to his book. I can't believe it. I look at Uncle Cliff. He can't believe it either.

'They're friendlier than they look, Matt,' says Mrs Jarvis.

'Come on, Matty,' says Uncle Cliff.

Matt gives us all a glare. Like we've been doing bad things behind his back.

'We just wanted to give you a happy surprise,' I say.

Matt doesn't say anything.

He definitely doesn't look happy.

'What's wrong, mate?' says Uncle Cliff.

'When you train with a top club,' says Matt, 'they don't want you playing football anywhere else.'

'They don't have to know,' says Mrs Jarvis. 'There'd be no harm done.'

'It's just a bit of fun,' I say.

Matt slams the book shut. I'm startled. You don't often see Matt angry.

'Don't you get it?' he says. 'I haven't got time for kid's stuff any more. I'm trying to be a Premier League footballer. I've got one chance in a thousand. I haven't got time to muck around.'

Me and Uncle Cliff and Mrs Jarvis don't know what to say.

But I understand. It must be terrible to feel that much pressure all the time. I'm lucky. I've got asthma. I have to take a break sometimes, just to start breathing again.

As we drive away, I see Matt glance one more time at the kids playing.

His face doesn't change. But because I'm his sister I can tell how much, deep down, he wants to be with them.

Which is why I'm going to do everything I can to get him onto that waste ground.

So he remembers what fun's like.

And how much of it we have at home.

32

At the training centre, Uncle Cliff and Mrs Jarvis go off to get a hot drink.

I watch Matt train.

So do the trainers and coaches. They're nodding and looking pleased. Matt is doing lots of skill.

The trainers might be pleased, but I'm not.

I can see how unhappy Matt is underneath the brilliance. I know exactly what he needs. And it's not a training session with a bunch of misery-guts who'll stretch your shirt or purposely splash mud on your shorts if they think it'll get them chosen for the first team before you.

Mum and Dad would probably think I'm being unfair, but they're not seeing what goes on here.

The person who looks most unhappy tonight is Ayo. I can see it even more clearly now the boys have split into two teams for a training match.

Matt plays brilliantly.

Two goals and no one can stop him.

Ayo isn't so good.

He doesn't just look unhappy, he looks angry. He's on the same team as Matt, which is just as well because he's being very rough with the other side.

Doing kicks carelessly.

Not caring who he bashes into.

Dad once worked with a bloke who thought if a doorway wasn't wide enough for a wardrobe, you could widen it.

Ayo is like that tonight.

At first the trainers don't seem to mind, but when Ayo lashes out with his elbow and leaves a boy lying down holding his ear and moaning that Ayo's broken it, they do mind.

They send Ayo off.

The other boys look a bit stunned. I don't think that happens much in training matches.

I watch Ayo leave the pitch. I feel sorry for him. I reckon he's like Matt. A good person who's under too much pressure.

I want to say something sympathetic to him, but he's walking very fast and his face is very angry. He's hurried past me by the time I realise he has tears on his face.

'Ayo,' I say.

I almost go after him. But then I see Mr Nkrumo walking over to meet him. A person should be allowed to have private time with their professional advisor. That's what I always used to feel if somebody tried to interrupt when I was talking about something important with Matt.

I hope Mr Nkrumo understands what Ayo is going through and gives him some sympathy or at least a hot drink.

The training match starts up again.

You'd think after somebody is sent off for violence, everyone else would keep a lid on things.

They don't.

If anything, they're playing grumpier and tougher than before. It's like they don't want to be left looking weak compared to Ayo.

Matt included.

I can hardly watch.

Matt slides into a tackle and the boy with the ball does half a somersault and hits the ground head first. I'm horrified. Matt never does sliding tackles from behind.

Or he didn't before he came here.

Matt needs the council estate urgently. And I reckon Ayo does too.

Hang on.

Of course.

Why didn't I think of that before?

If Ayo was playing with the estate kids, Matt might feel better about doing it himself. For a start, he wouldn't be the only one breaking the rules.

I look around to see if Ayo is still here.

He's over by the minibus, talking to Mr Nkrumo.

I start to hurry over to them, then stop.

It's probably best if Mr Nkrumo doesn't know about this. I think Mr Nkrumo takes rules a bit seriously. I need to have a chat with Ayo when he's on his own.

I know the best place to do that, and I don't hesitate. I head straight into the boys' changing room.

33

Hiding here in Ayo's locker probably isn't the best idea I've ever had.

I did it in case training finishes and the rest of the boys come into the changing room before Ayo does. That way at least I'll be hidden and I can have a chat with Ayo through the door.

That's if I'm not unconscious.

It's not Ayo's fault. Everyone's locker probably smells like this. It's natural with all the sweaty socks and pongy deodorants that get stored in them.

I concentrate on keeping my breathing good.

Mum and Dad, I wish you could see this. It's what I've been trying to tell you. Even in tricky and slightly smelly situations I can look after myself.

What's that sound?

It's soccer studs clacking on the floor.

That's a relief. Ayo must have finished his chat with Mr Nkrumo and come in here to get changed early so he doesn't have face the other boys after being sent off.

I'll just gently open the locker door so I don't startle him too much, and we can have a little chat.

Except the locker door won't open.

There's no handle this side. When it swung shut behind me I didn't notice that. I can't believe it. What idiot would design a locker with a door that can't be opened from the inside?

OK, Mum and Dad, if you were here now you'd be seeing that even when situations get slightly trickier, I still don't panic. Even though there's just a chance Ayo got into the minibus with Mr Nkrumo to get changed at home and it's somebody else who's come into the changing room and they've got earphones in and won't hear me and I could be discovered next week as a skeleton.

I'm still not panicking. Not totally.

Someone pulls the door open.

Relax Mum and Dad, it is Ayo.

Eeuw. Why would a person take all their clothes off before they open their locker?

'Sorry,' I say.

'Arghhh,' yells Ayo.

He grabs his soccer shirt and wraps it round his waist.

I'm not too shocked. You're not when you've had older brothers and parents who are too busy for weeks on end to fix the lock on the bathroom door.

'What you doing?' Ayo yells at me.

'I just wanted a chat,' I say, stepping out of the locker.

'I know you,' says Ayo. 'You're Matt's sister. You a maniac or what, girl?'

I'm tempted to point out that he's the one who's just been sent off for unruly behaviour. But I don't. Instead I ask him if he remembers how much fun soccer used to be when he was a kid.

Ayo stares at me like I'm talking another language.

'You know,' I say. 'Kick-arounds in the street or next to the cattle yard or in the supermarket car park.'

'No supermarket,' says Ayo. 'Not in my village. I'm West Africa, not West Bromwich.'

I ask him if his village is affected by wombats.

He says no over his shoulder as he puts his shorts on. Then he starts to relax as we talk about how wildlife can make soccer even more interesting.

'Do you miss it?' I say. 'Where you grew up?'

Ayo thinks. And nods a bit unhappily.

I tell him about the council estate.

'It's kind of like a village,' I say. 'No elephants, not that I know about. But fun.'

'Matt,' says Ayo. 'He playing there too?'

'That's the plan,' I say.

'Against the rules, though,' says Ayo.

'That's why you mustn't tell Mr Nkrumo,' I say. 'Come over to Mrs Jarvis's and we'll take you.'

Ayo thinks about this. I can see he likes the idea of doing something without Mr Nkrumo breathing down his neck.

'Maybe,' he says. He grins. 'Alright, it's a plan.'

Brilliant.

I give him a high handshake.

Then not so brilliant.

All the other boys come in.

It's a bit chaotic for a while, but you'd be pleased to see, Mum and Dad, that I handle it pretty well. I apologise to them all, and warn them about the lack of handles on the inside of their locker doors.

While I'm doing that, and Ayo is flicking some of the rude ones with a towel, I notice that Matt isn't in the changing room yet, so I hurry outside to find him.

He's over by the pitch talking to Uncle Cliff and Mrs Jarvis. Terrine is with them, but not Gazz.

'Hi Bridie,' says Terrine. 'I've been hearing how well Matt's doing.'

'The trainers are very happy,' says Mrs Jarvis.

'Pure rock 'n' roll,' says Uncle Cliff. 'Home-sickness, constipation, nothing slows him down.'

Matt looks a bit embarrassed. I don't blame him.

'Thanks for the tea the other day, girls,' Terrine says to me and Mrs Jarvis. 'Got to go now. We've got fourteen for dinner and one of them's a royal.'

We say goodbye and watch Terrine get into her yellow Lamborghini.

Matt can't take his eyes off it.

I bet he's thinking of buying one for Mum. I know she wouldn't want it. Not if it cost her the only son she's got left. I reckon if she knew, she'd say I'm doing the right thing here.

I hope.

'Poor Terrine,' says Mrs Jarvis. 'Gazz sends her down here to check up on the trainees. Make sure none of them looks like taking his job this week.'

'Gazz sounds really stressed,' says Uncle Cliff. 'I should offer to lend him my iPod. It's got some really relaxing Grateful Dead on it.'

'What Terrine really wishes,' I say, 'is that Gazz could rediscover the joyful spirit of the beautiful game. And play football as football should be played. Like he used to, growing up on his council estate.'

I think I got all the words in the right order.

I look at Matt.

Matt doesn't say anything.

'Which is a coincidence,' I say. 'I was just talking to Ayo and he grew up on a council estate.'

Uncle Cliff and Mrs Jarvis give me a look.

'Sort of a council estate,' I say. 'It was more like an African village really, but Ayo's very keen to have a game on the estate here. I think he's feeling lonely being so far from home.'

'Nice kids on that estate,' says Mrs Jarvis. 'He'll have fun.'

Matt is frowning.

'It's against the rules,' he says.

Mrs Jarvis gives Matt the sort of look she often gives Uncle Cliff.

'Matt,' she says. 'Breaking rules is like breaking wind. You don't do it all the time, but occasionally you have to.'

Uncle Cliff gazes at her. He's definitely in love.

Mrs Jarvis leans towards Matt and speaks in a whisper.

'I'm not meant to make fishcakes,' she says. 'They're not on the club diet. But I do because Mr Merchant likes me to bring them in for him sometimes.'

She gives Matt a naughty grin.

Matt looks doubtful for a moment, then grins back.

34

When we arrive at the council estate, there are about ten kids already having a kick-around.

I get out of the car first. Lola is pleased to see me and wants me to go in goal again, which is really nice of her.

'Not today, thanks,' I say.

For a moment I think Lola is going to argue, but then she meets Matt and Ayo and gets distracted.

I'm feeling too stressed to go in goal. I know I'm not a manager any more, but sometimes it's just as stressful being a sister. Specially when you're trying to save your brother and he doesn't even want to be saved.

While Uncle Cliff gives some of the estate kids high-up handshakes to show how friendly we Aussies are, Mrs Jarvis gives me a quick squeeze.

'You've done all you can,' she says. 'It's up to Matt now.'

I know she's right. But I wish there was an easier way of saving him. Hypnotism or something.

The game starts up again with Matt and Ayo playing one on each side.

Matt starts having fun almost straight away.

Me and Uncle Cliff and Mrs Jarvis grin at each other. It's so good seeing Matt doing cartwheels down the whole length of the council estate pitch after the goal he set up was booted in by a boy in a Chelsea shirt. Who's blowing him kisses.

A couple of times Ayo forgets the difference between a game and a match and grabs other kids' shirts. Uncle Cliff gives him a whistle from the sideline and Ayo remembers and lets go and says sorry.

When Ayo is relaxed, he plays really well. Skilful and fast. Not as skilful and fast as Matt, but almost. I can see why he was the top under-fifteen player before Matt came along.

It's starting to get dark.

The estate kids don't seem to care. They play on in the gloom. When they can't see the ball or each other, they just laugh more.

Uncle Cliff turns the car headlights on and aims them towards the pitch.

'Thanks,' yells a boy in an army greatcoat.

He gets tackled by Ayo. Who gets tackled by Matt. Good clever tackling without any holding, turning or elbows.

Which is why the angry car horn we hear, loud

and going on and on, seems a bit out of place.

'Who's that?' says Mrs Jarvis, peering at a pair of headlights flashing towards us.

I recognise the vehicle. Mr Nkrumo's minibus.

It drives off the road and onto the pitch, horn still blaring angrily.

'Hey,' yells Uncle Cliff. 'We're having a game here.'

The minibus stops in the middle of the pitch and Mr Nkrumo gets out. He yells at Ayo. Ayo stares at him, shoulders slumping. Mr Nkrumo yells even more angrily. Stuff about how Ayo is a very stupid boy. Ayo walks slowly over to the minibus. Mr Nkrumo pushes him inside, glares at us, gets in and drives away.

As the minibus revs past us, I see Ayo's sad face against the glass, his eyes closed.

We're all a bit stunned.

'Is it his bedtime?' says one of the younger boys.

I can see Matt looking concerned. About Ayo, but maybe also wondering if he's being a stupid boy himself.

'Come on,' I say to them all. 'Don't let dopey old Mr Nkrumo spoil the fun.'

'That's right,' says Uncle Cliff. 'I'll have a word with him at training tomorrow. Tell him he's not doing Ayo any favours, behaving like a prawn.'

Mrs Jarvis doesn't say anything.

She keeps glancing down the street in the direction the minibus took. I know how she feels.

Poor Ayo.

'Come on, Matt,' says Lola. 'Your sister's right. Play on.'

Matt plays on. But it's not the same.

He tries to be fair. He doesn't score for several minutes. And when he does it's with his left foot. While he's lying on the ground.

'Yes,' yells the boy in the Chelsea shirt, who's happy because he's on Matt's side.

'Fluke,' yells the boy in the army coat, who's not.

'Matt,' I say. 'Time to change sides.'

'Hang on,' protests the boy in the Chelsea shirt. 'We don't change sides here.'

'Yes we do,' says the boy in the army coat. 'When Liam used to play with us he changed sides all the time.'

'He was three,' says Lola. 'He didn't know what a side was.'

All the other kids start arguing and nobody listens to me as I try to explain how changing sides is perfectly normal in Australia. Matt tries too, but they ignore him as well. The argument just gets worse, right up to the moment the yellow Lamborghini arrives.

Then nobody says anything.

We all just stare as the Lamborghini parks next to Uncle Cliff's car.

Me and Matt and Uncle Cliff and Mrs Jarvis are a bit more prepared than the others for what happens next. So we don't actually do any squeaks or say any Horns And Tail Hotel words when one of the most famous footballers in the world gets out of the Lamborghini with his beautiful girlfriend.

'Flippin heck, Terrine,' says Gazz. 'It's a bleedin' estate.'

'So what,' says Terrine. 'Don't be rude. Anyway, you had fun growing up on yours, you're always telling journalists that.'

Gazz isn't sure what to say.

He glances at Mrs Jarvis, who's smiling at him.

Then he sees all the open mouths and all the big eyes staring at him.

''Allo, kids,' he says.

'Wotcha,' Terrine says to the rest of us. 'Thanks for suggesting this, Mrs J. It's just what Gazz needs.'

Gazz is walking onto the pitch, giving a car parts hole a wary kick.

'You'd have to be well skilled to play on this,' he says.

'That's lucky,' says Terrine. 'Cos you are.'

Gazz flips the ball into the air with his foot and does some ball juggling with his knees, shoulders and head.

'Come on then,' he says to the kids. 'Tackle me.'

Nobody moves.

'They don't know whose side you're on, you wally,' says Terrine.

The boy in the army coat clears his throat. He does it several times before any words come out.

'We need an extra player on our side,' he croaks.

163

'Is that right?' says Gazz.

'Yeah,' says Matt, stepping out from behind the other kids. 'They do.'

Gazz looks at Matt.

''Allo, Nipper,' he says. 'So this is your secret, eh? This is where you get it all from. Dribbling round the old car parts, eh?'

I can see Matt isn't sure what to say.

'Gazz,' says Terrine. 'Be nice.'

'Given this one'll be wearing my shirt in a few months,' Gazz says, ruffling Matt's hair, 'I think I'm being very nice. OK, which way am I kicking?'

The game starts again.

At first nobody wants to tackle Gazz. Matt shows them how. Even I hold my breath the first time he does it. But an amazing thing happens. Gazz doesn't mind. Well, he does, but not in a cross grown-up way. In a laughing kid way.

Then Lola and the others tackle him too. You can see they can hardly believe what their feet are doing. But only for the first couple of minutes. Then it's just a normal game, only with slightly more dazzling footwork and a couple of players who are a bit better than the others, but just as hopeless when they laugh too much.

Uncle Cliff's headlights start to fade, so Terrine switches theirs on instead.

I'm not kidding, a Lamborghini lights up a soccer pitch better than the floodlights at Wembley stadium.

Mrs Jarvis puts her arm round me, and Uncle Cliff puts his arm round her.

The kids play on, giggling and falling about, with Gazz the biggest happiest kid of all and Matt not far behind.

After a bit, Mrs Jarvis sighs and shakes her head.

'Why would anyone give all this up,' she murmurs, 'for a measly two hundred thousand pounds a week?'

Terrine nods sadly.

I don't think Uncle Cliff heard her, because a few minutes later, after he finishes cheering a goal, he turns to me.

'This plan of yours is Judas H brilliant,' he says. 'Matt's happier than a pig in porridge. Now he's cheered up, I reckon he'll crack a place in the first team before you can say fat wallet.'

I don't reply.

I glance at Mrs Jarvis and Terrine. They don't say anything either.

But I can see we're all hoping Uncle Cliff is wrong.

35

'I reckon I'm right,' says Uncle Cliff at training. 'Matt's a new bloke after that kick-around on the estate last night.'

Mrs Jarvis gives him a look.

'I don't think he is, Cliff,' she says. 'It takes between two and seventeen years for the cells in the human body to be renewed, not one night.'

Uncle Cliff gazes at her adoringly.

I gaze at Matt miserably.

The council estate kick-around didn't work. Matt hasn't gone back to his old self. He's still grim-faced and training hard like he wants to be the one. Still holding and turning and elbowing as much as the others.

He told me he enjoyed the kick-around, but he can't do it again because it'll make him soft.

'Go, Matty,' yells Uncle Cliff as Matt does a sliding tackle into somebody from behind.

I don't think Matt's even noticed that Ayo isn't at training today.

'Aussie leg pins,' says Uncle Cliff as Matt scrambles to his feet. 'Best in the world.'

'Oh dear,' says Mrs Jarvis, squinting at something.

She takes my arm and points at Mr Nkrumo's minibus driving past.

I catch a glimpse of Ayo in the back, eyes down, face miserable.

'Ayo,' I call.

But he doesn't hear me, and the bus zooms towards the exit gate.

'I've got a bad feeling about this,' says Mrs Jarvis. 'I think it's time I had another chat with Mr Merchant.'

Uncle Cliff isn't listening to her.

'Don't look,' he says, wincing. 'Matt just elbowed somebody in that really sensitive spot just inside the penalty area.'

Too late.

I saw it.

This is a tragedy.

And I don't know what to do.

36

Something's happening that's as unexpected as the chilli in Mrs Jarvis's cheese and chilli omelette.

The others are so busy they haven't seen it yet.

Mrs Jarvis is busy cooking Uncle Cliff an extra treat because he ate all his omelette. It's a kipper, which is a kind of smoked fish with a flat face. Uncle Cliff is busy gazing at Mrs Jarvis like he is the kipper.

Matt is busy flipping an egg between his feet.

I'm busy gazing out the window wondering how I can get Matt back onto the estate for another chance at happiness.

Which is how come I see it.

'Oh,' says Mrs Jarvis. 'Look at that.'

At first I think she's seen it as well. The big black car pulling up outside the house. But she's talking about something else. The beads of chilli sweat running down the side of Uncle Cliff's face.

'It's very black,' says Mrs Jarvis.

'I think it's a Bentley,' says Matt, who's just seen the car.

'I'm talking about Cliff's perspiration,' says Mrs Jarvis. 'Do you dye your hair, Cliff?'

'Not dye exactly,' says Uncle Cliff, mopping his face. 'The box says it's colour enhancement.'

'Look,' I say urgently, pointing out the window. Uncle Cliff and Mrs Jarvis look.

A uniformed driver is getting out of the big black car and coming to the house.

We hurry to the front door.

'Good morning,' says the driver. 'Mr Jean-Pierre Michel would like to see Miss Sutherland in his office as soon as possible.'

We stare at him.

I realise Miss Sutherland is me.

'Have I got time to finish my kipper?' says Uncle Cliff.

We're all in the car in about ten minutes. The driver says he doesn't know what it's about.

'I just drive,' he says. 'And sometimes pick up Mr Michel's duck sandwiches.'

'Maybe the club wants you to be a mascot again,' says Uncle Cliff to me.

Mrs Jarvis gives him a look.

I don't say what I hope it's about. How I hope the staff at the academy have noticed Matt doesn't seem very happy. And how Jean-Pierre Michel is wondering if there's anything he can do to help.

'Yes,' I'll say. 'There is something actually.' Then I'll ask him to please book us some plane tickets home *immediatement*, which is French for pronto.

We arrive at the stadium.

Jean-Pierre Michel's secretary meets us and takes us to Mr Michel's office.

'Just the young lady,' she says. 'The rest of you please wait here.'

While Uncle Cliff and Mrs Jarvis and Matt sit in the outer office next to a cardboard cut-out of Gazz, the secretary takes me into the inner office.

'Hello, Bridie,' says Jean-Pierre Michel, standing up and brushing crumbs off his suit. 'Thanks for coming. Would you like a croissant or a brioche?'

I think that's food. I explain to him we've just had chilli omelette.

Jean-Pierre Michel asks me to sit down. Then he tells me that last night the club played Ajax in the European Champions League and won four–nil. Which is the first match they've won in five weeks.

I'm not sure what to say.

It's good and everything, but he didn't have to bring me here to tell me that. I would have heard it on the news.

'Best of all,' says Jean-Pierre Michel, 'we had a hat-trick. A wonderful return to form by a player who's been seriously off-form for several months. A player who, the evening before, visited you and your brother. I think you know who I mean.'

I'm still not sure what to say.

Mr Michel must have found out about Gazz playing with the estate kids. Are me and Matt and Uncle Cliff and Mrs Jarvis in trouble? Is Jean-Pierre Michel cross that his forty-three-million-pound player could have fallen into a car-part hole?

He doesn't look cross.

While I'm feeling confused, Mr Michel comes round from behind his desk and sits in a chair next to mine.

'The first time you were in this office,' he says, 'you told me about fun.'

I remember. He wasn't that impressed.

'Tell me again,' he says. 'Tell me about fun. Because last night I saw that a certain player was having a lot of fun.'

'Well,' I say, and I take a deep breath and tell him about the council estate game, and the friendliness of it, and the no violence, and how much laughing there is, and how big Lola's handbag is, and how much better people play when they're happy.

'And,' I say, 'if your stadium lights ever pack up, I'd use Lamborghinis.'

Jean-Pierre Michel nods thoughtfully.

'Of course,' he says, almost to himself. 'That's where Gazz started out. Fun kick-arounds on a council estate.'

'Everybody starts with fun kick-arounds,' I say. 'Every soccer star in the world was a kid once. Having fun. That's why they want to do it as a job.'

Jean-Pierre Michel thinks about this.

'What about the ten million pounds a year?' he says.

'That's good too,' I say. 'But not if you're so worried and miserable that you can't even enjoy a simple waterfall.'

We talk lots more.

When we say goodbye, Mr Michel gives me a look. It's a very different look to the one he gave me last time I was in his office.

'Thank you,' he says.

I go into the outer office. Uncle Cliff and Mrs Jarvis and Matt all jump up anxiously.

'What happened?' says Uncle Cliff. 'Is everything OK?'

I grin at them all, specially Matt, because I think this is going to be very OK for him.

'Everything's fine,' I say. 'Mr Michel has given me a job at the academy.'

37

'**A** job?' says Mum, when we Skype them with the news.

'It's more of a consultancy,' says Uncle Cliff.

'It's a thousand pounds a week,' says Matt.

Mum and Dad look stunned.

'Not a week,' I say. 'Mr Michel gave me a thousand pounds for reminding him about something.'

'What?' says Dad.

'How soccer stars were all kids once,' I say. 'And how if they remember that, they'll have more fun playing top-level professional football in the first part of the twenty-first century. And they'll probably score more goals.'

'That sounds reasonable,' says Mum.

'Mr Michel wants all his players to remember it,' I say. 'He's told them if they don't, he'll sell them.'

'Thanks to your daughter,' says Mrs Jarvis, joining in, 'the club's decided to try a different way of doing things. It's Judas H amazing.'

Mrs Jarvis is right, it is.

When we get to training, all the goalposts and nets have been taken down. Six-a-side games are being played all over the training pitches with piles of tracksuit tops as goalposts and academy kids all mixed up together with first-team players and everyone laughing and doing skill and accepting a hand up if they fall over.

OK, not quite everyone. A few people look a bit confused but not many.

Mr Merchant is the only one who looks totally unhappy.

'Hello, Neal,' says Mrs Jarvis. 'You still haven't got back to me about Ayo.'

I look around and realise Ayo isn't here.

Mr Merchant, who was glaring at me, glares at Mrs Jarvis instead.

'I suggest you go to the horse's mouth,' he says. 'Mr Nkrumo will tell you about Ayodele Awolopo.'

He walks off.

Mrs Jarvis watches him go for a moment. I think she might be considering a sliding tackle from behind.

But instead she turns to me and Uncle Cliff.

'I'm going to find Mr Nkrumo,' she says. 'See you later.'

I'm worried about Ayo too, but I wish Mrs Jarvis could stay for a while. It's so great, watching Matt and Gazz playing together again. And is that . . . yes, it's Jean-Pierre Michel playing with them in a very flashy tracksuit.

'Rock 'n' roll,' says Uncle Cliff, gazing around. 'This is like six-a-side Woodstock.'

I don't actually know what Woodstock is, but I do know Matt's got a big grin on his face, even though he just missed an overhead kick.

Everyone's got big grins on their faces.

This probably won't stop them busting a gut to be the one, or to win the league, but in future they might be a bit nicer about it. And their hearts might not end up so hard and unhappy.

Matt's included.

Everyone takes a short break for drinks and leg massages.

After a bit, Matt comes over to me and Uncle Cliff. I've never seen him so excited and happy.

'Guess what Mr Michel just told me,' he says.

'He's got tickets for the Stones concert next week in Paris?' says Uncle Cliff.

'He's putting me in the first team on Saturday,' says Matt.

We stare at Matt, gobsmacked.

'The first team?' I say.

'The first first team?' says Uncle Cliff.

'Against Chelsea,' says Matt.

'You're sure you haven't got that wrong,' says Uncle Cliff. 'You're sure you're not a bit dazed after that overhead kick.'

Matt shakes his head.

He does look a little bit dazed, but not from the overhead kick. We all probably look a bit dazed.

Jean-Pierre Michel comes over and puts his hand on Matt's shoulder.

'When Matt runs out into the stadium on Saturday,' he says, 'it will remind the rest of the team of their own childhoods. Of why they play this game. And of course it will be very good publicity for the club. The youngest player ever in the Premier League. On Saturday, Matt will be the most famous boy in the world.'

'Judas H,' says Uncle Cliff.

Matt gives me a grin.

I give him one back.

And I make a decision. I'm going to send my thousand pounds to Mum and Dad. So they can buy some warm clothes. For when they come to England.

38

When we get back to the house, Mrs Jarvis meets us at the front door.

She looks grim.

'We've got a visitor,' she says.

She takes me and Matt and Uncle Cliff into the lounge room and we see who the visitor is.

Mr Nkrumo. He's sitting with a cup of tea, looking grim too. And upset. And sort of anxious.

We all sit down.

'You'd better start at the beginning again please, Mr Nkrumo,' says Mrs Jarvis.

Mr Nkrumo looks like he wishes he was somewhere else. I'm glad he's here. I want to know what's happened to Ayo.

'We're Ayo's friends,' I say. 'We want to help.'

Mr Nkrumo suddenly looks cross.

'Just because Ayo is an African boy,' he says, 'everybody thinks Ayo needs help.'

'He does need help, you daft pillock,' says Mrs Jarvis, 'And the reason he needs it is you.'

I'm shocked by the tone of her voice.

Mr Nkrumo sags.

'Ayo is being released,' says Mrs Jarvis.

She must know what that means because she's looking really upset.

'What's released?' I say.

'The club is sending Ayo home,' says Mr Nkrumo. 'They don't want him any more.'

I'm shocked. I look at Uncle Cliff and Matt. They are too.

'Poor Ayo,' I say. 'That's terrible.'

'It gets worse,' says Mrs Jarvis. 'Tell Bridie and Matt and Cliff what you told the club, Mr Nkrumo.'

'I told them that Ayo comes from the poorest part of Nigeria,' says Mr Nkrumo. 'His village is at the mercy of everything. Bandits, disease, drought.'

I nod. I know about drought.

'Every few years,' says Mr Nkrumo, 'when the drought comes, many people die in the village.'

I stare at him. I don't know about that sort of drought.

Mrs Jarvis and Matt and Uncle Cliff are staring at him too. Mrs Jarvis is biting her lip.

'A wonderful thing happened to the village,' says Mr Nkrumo miserably. 'A boy was taken to England. To play football. To earn money. So that when the drought comes, his village can buy water.'

I don't know what to say.

Yes I do.

'This isn't fair,' I say. 'Ayo's a good player. Plus he's kind. He shouldn't be forced to go home just because all the stress made him a bit violent and he got sent off.'

Mr Nkrumo hesitates. He sees Mrs Jarvis looking at him.

'Ayo isn't being sent home because he got violent,' says Mr Nkrumo. 'He's being sent home because what I just told you isn't true.'

I gape at him.

'I made it all up about the village,' says Mr Nkrumo miserably. 'To make the club feel sympathy for Ayo and give him a better chance.'

'But it wasn't really for Ayo, was it?' says Mrs Jarvis. 'How much of Ayo's future salary do you get as his manager?'

'Eighty percent,' says Mr Nkrumo in a small voice.

I'm stunned.

I can see Uncle Cliff and Matt are as well.

'But,' says Matt, 'Ayo told me about his village himself.'

'Ayo comes from the city of Nairobi,' says Mr Nkrumo. 'I made him tell the village story. I told him if he didn't, I would send him home. But he told the club it was a lie, and now the club is sending him home.'

Nobody says anything for a while.

We're all just taking this in.

Poor Ayo. It's not fair. A person shouldn't have their dream shattered just because of a manager.

'I feel very bad,' says Mr Nkrumo. 'I've come here today because you are Ayo's friends. I'm hoping there's some way you can help Ayo.'

'Help Ayo,' says Mrs Jarvis, 'or help you?'

'It is true,' says Mr Nkrumo, 'that the club has said they won't consider any of my young clients in future. Unless perhaps you, Mrs Jarvis, could have a kind word with your friend Mr Merchant.'

'I've had a word with Mr Merchant,' says Mrs Jarvis grimly. 'Mr Pig-Headed Merchant says they won't change their mind about Ayo or you.'

Mr Nkrumo sags.

The rest of us look at each other.

Ayo's the one we're worried about.

Of course we want to help him, but how?

39

'**G**o on strike?' says Matt.

He's totally horrified. He stares at me. There's a lump of fishcake on his fork that's he's completely forgotten about. That's how I know how horrified he is.

'Not exactly go on strike,' I say, wishing I'd thought of a different word. 'Just tell Jean-Pierre Michel you won't play in the first team tomorrow unless Ayo's in the team too. So Ayo has another chance to show what a good player he is. Too good to send home.'

Matt is frowning, elbows on the table. He's still not seeing the positives we can take out of this.

'It's like what Mum did at the factory,' I say. 'When the manager wouldn't fix the wiring. She got all the others to agree. No work until they were given sewing machines that didn't, um . . .'

I can't think of the word.

181

'Short out,' says Uncle Cliff. 'It's an electrical term.'

He glances at Mrs Jarvis to see if she's impressed.

'Unusual,' says Mrs Jarvis. 'Sewing machines usually have a two-phase step-down capacitor that overrides short circuits with a rotating oscillator field.'

Uncle Cliff gazes at Mrs Jarvis, like I imagine he would if the real Mick Jagger walked into the room.

I try to get through to Matt.

'It's just helping others in a friendly way,' I say. 'It's what we always do. Mum had a different word for it, but it's the same thing.'

'Solidarity,' says Uncle Cliff.

'Good word,' says Mrs Jarvis.

Uncle Cliff glows.

Matt puts his fork down so hard two Brussels sprouts jump off the table. He doesn't flip them back up with his feet like he usually would.

'I'm not hungry,' he says. 'I'm going to my room.'

He goes.

I get up to follow him.

Uncle Cliff puts his fork down.

'I'll come too,' he says.

'Your choice, Cliff,' says Mrs Jarvis, picking up the brussels sprouts. 'But you'll miss out on the chance to come into the kitchen and help me wash up.'

She gives Uncle Cliff a look.

Uncle Cliff hesitates. Mrs Jarvis looks at me and

flicks her eyes towards the door. She knows that some conversations are best between a soccer star and his sister.

I hurry upstairs.

Matt is in his room, but not on his bed flipping something between his feet like I'd expected.

He's standing up, staring out the window.

'Ayo's our friend,' I say. 'We always help our friends.'

Matt turns to me and grabs my shoulders.

I'm shocked. He's never done that before. It doesn't hurt or anything. It's just that Matt's more the egg-flipping type.

'I can't,' he says. 'I can't risk losing my chance.'

It's almost like he's pleading with me.

'Ayo's your friend,' I say.

I don't know how else to put it.

Matt takes his hands off my shoulders and stares at the floor. His face goes so determined it's like Gazz's ancient Greek goalie that's made of stone.

'Mr Merchant told us something at training the other day,' says Matt. 'He said that friends are a luxury. Because getting to the top is hard. And friends make you soft.'

I can see how much Matt is struggling to believe it. His eyes are almost as big as Lamborghini headlights.

Suddenly I want to cry.

Matt looks like he does too.

I put my arms round him and hold him tight.

My face is pressed into his chest. This is the closest I've been to him for ages. I can feel my tears wetting his shirt.

'I'm sorry,' he says.

I can't speak. But if I could, I'd tell him I'm sorry too. Because it was my job to protect him from all this. My job as a manager and a sister.

And I've failed.

40

We Skype Mum and Dad to tell them about Matt's success. About him playing in the first team tomorrow. And how the club wants him to stay on for another month.

Mum and Dad tell Matt how proud and excited they are, and how much they wish they could be there in person.

'Thanks,' says Matt.

Mum blows him a kiss.

'The club wants to fly both of you over as soon as you can come,' says Mrs Jarvis. 'They'll arrange some help for your old folk while you're away.'

Mum and Dad say they'll be here in a couple of weeks, three tops.

I'm not saying much.

I don't want Mum and Dad to see how in despair I am.

Mum frowns.

'Isn't it a bit dangerous,' she says. 'A fourteen-year-old playing with grown-ups?'

'He's been doing it all day in training,' says Uncle Cliff. 'We haven't had the first-aid kit out once.'

'To be honest, love,' says Mrs Jarvis to Mum, 'there are risks. But Matt is a very skilful player. He knows how to look after himself.'

'Stella's right,' says Uncle Cliff. 'I mean Mrs Jarvis is.'

Mrs Jarvis rolls her eyes at Mum and Dad.

'Cliff,' she says. 'You're a grown man with your own hair concept. You're allowed to call me Stella.'

Mum and Dad laugh.

'Matt'll be fine,' says Uncle Cliff. 'Specially with Bridie looking after him.'

I try to smile.

'We're proud of you, Matt,' says Mum.

'We are,' says Dad. 'Very. Oh, and Cliff, great photos on your Facebook, mate. All those ones of the big mansion and the yellow Lamborghini, very interesting. But not many of Bridie and Matt. Can you give us more of them?'

'Please,' says Mum.

'Right-o,' says Uncle Cliff.

'Don't stress too much,' says Matt to Uncle Cliff. 'They've got heaps of photos of Bridie and me at home.'

Uncle Cliff gives him a look.

'I think what they're saying, Matty,' he says, 'is that they care about you and Bridie about a million times more than they care about rich clobber.'

Mum and Dad nod.

'Well put, Cliff,' says Mrs Jarvis.

I look at Matt.

He's staring at the floor. I'm not sure if he's even paying attention any more.

After we say goodbye to Mum and Dad, there's more Skyping to do. Lots more people from home want to say congratulations and good luck to Matt.

Jayden, Zac, Celine, Callum and Gael-Anne are all at Celine's place.

'Score a hat-trick,' says Celine.

'Two,' says Jayden.

Even a couple of the orange team want to say g'day.

'Go in hard,' says the orange captain.

He means well.

While Matt is thanking them all, I see at the bottom of the screen it says that 28,659,822 people are on Skype right now. I wonder how many of them are feeling as proud and excited as Mum and Dad and our friends.

Probably not many.

I wish I was.

41

The stadium is even noisier than when I was a mascot.

A humungous thundering wave of noise that Uncle Cliff says is louder than being right down the front at a Stones concert the day after you've had your ears syringed specially.

And we're not even up in the stadium yet.

We're outside the first-team changing room, giving Matt a hug.

He doesn't want us to. The other first-team players are all inside and none of them have got sisters or uncles or landladies hugging them.

'Be careful,' says Mrs Jarvis.

'Break a leg,' says Uncle Cliff, giving Matt a wink.

'I'll be fine,' says Matt.

'You'll be brilliant,' I say.

And I mean it. This is Matt's big day and I'm trying my hardest not to feel bad and selfishly spoil it just because he's turned into somebody else.

Jean-Pierre Michel arrives.

'OK Matt,' he says, 'time for the pre-match team talk. Don't be put off if they're not very pleased to see you at first.'

Mr Michel gives us all a smile, which looks to me like a slightly nervous one, and takes Matt into the changing room.

Uncle Cliff and Mrs Jarvis have a sudden need to go to the toilet. Stress can do that to people over thirty.

While they're gone I slump against a wall and try not to think about Matt going through the rest of his life without any friends. Except maybe a big fierce dog if he gets desperate.

Somebody taps me on the shoulder.

It's Ayo.

'Hello,' I say, surprised and happy and concerned all at once.

There's heaps I want to say, to try and help him feel better, but I don't know how.

'Just want to say goodbye,' says Ayo. 'I'm going tomorrow and I just want to say sorry too. Bad story I spun, that one.'

'It's OK,' I say. 'Mr Nkrumo explained. It wasn't your fault.'

'Still feel bad,' says Ayo.

I try to see on his face if he knows. That Matt could have tried to help him. And didn't.

'Have you seen Matt?' I say.

Ayo shakes his head.

'Just come to see him play on his big day,' he says. 'Better go find a seat.'

'If you want, you can sit with us,' I say.

'Thanks,' says Ayo. 'If I can't find nothing.'

He shakes my hand.

'Sweet dreams, girl,' he says.

'Bye,' I say. 'Good luck.'

Ayo heads off and a few moments later Uncle Cliff and Mrs Jarvis come back.

'Was that Ayo?' says Mrs Jarvis.

I nod sadly.

'Poor boy,' she says.

'I've been thinking,' says Uncle Cliff. 'What if I offer him my iPod to take back to Africa?'

'Is it a recent model?' says Mrs Jarvis.

'Recent-ish,' says Uncle Cliff, holding it out.

Mrs Jarvis looks at it. I see her notice the bit of chewing gum on the top to make the earphones work. She shakes her head.

Uncle Cliff sags a bit and puts it away.

Mrs Jarvis puts her hand on his arm.

'You're a good man, Cliff,' she says quietly. 'There should be more like you.'

I give his hand a squeeze. Mrs Jarvis is right. If everybody had an uncle as kind as Uncle Cliff, the world would be a better place, and I don't care if the Australian media quotes me on that.

We go up to our VIP box in the stadium. I've never heard noise and excitement like it. Jean-Pierre

Michel is a publicity genius. Put one *Guinness Book Of Records* kid in your team and the whole world goes bananas.

Double bananas when the teams come out.

I can see the Chelsea players glancing at Matt like they didn't fully believe he'd actually be here until this moment.

What a moment.

Uncle Cliff and Mrs Jarvis have both got tears in their eyes. I'm desperately trying to keep mine dry. So I don't miss a thing. So I can tell Mum and Dad everything, specially the bits they don't see on TV or online.

Everything about the day their son's dream is finally coming true.

Except I don't know if I'm the right person to tell them. Because this is also the day my dream is going down the toilet. My dream of saving my last remaining brother.

Just before kick-off, Ayo comes into our box.

'No seats,' he says apologetically.

'You're very welcome,' says Mrs Jarvis, patting the empty seat next to her.

The match starts quietly.

It's as if, with a fourteen-year-old playing and so many people round the world watching, both teams want to be on their best behaviour.

None of our players pass to Matt at first, and he hangs back a bit, getting a feel for the game. But slowly he starts to get involved, just small touches.

The game speeds up, but friendly and clean and good-hearted.

Even when Chelsea score, the mood in the stadium stays friendly. Mostly. There are a few thousand fans who want to kill Jean-Pierre Michel for putting a kid in the team, but they don't actually do it.

After a while, I think Matt hears their yells.

Suddenly, about twenty minutes in, he starts to really play. Intercepting passes. Doing runs. Setting up goals.

'Beautiful run,' yells Uncle Cliff. 'Exquisite set-up.'

But he doesn't yell anything after that because there's something wrong.

Three times Matt does it.

He takes the ball past loads of defenders, moving his body like one of those clothes-drying racks that fold in all directions, and each time he gets close to the goal, he passes the ball into an empty space.

Where no one is.

Each time he does that, he looks straight across at Jean-Pierre Michel, who's standing near the touchline, then over at us in our box.

No, not at us, at Ayo.

After the second time, I realise what he's doing.

So does Mrs Jarvis.

'He's telling them that if Ayo was playing,' she says, 'Ayo would have scored just then.'

'Judas H incredible,' whispers Uncle Cliff.

But it gets even more incredible.

After Matt passes into an empty space for the third time, and players in his team are scowling at him, and Gazz is pleading with him, and Chelsea are laughing at him, Jean-Pierre Michel starts yelling at him.

We can't hear what Mr Michel is saying from up here, but we can tell from his wild hand movements.

'Shots, Sutherland,' he's saying. 'Shots from you or you're off.'

Matt obeys him.

A couple of minutes later he dances the ball to the edge of the Chelsea penalty area and shoots. It's less than twenty metres. I've never seen Matt miss from that close. But his shot slams into the left-hand goalpost and spins away for a goal kick.

'Bad luck,' groans Uncle Cliff and about thirty thousand other fans.

This is strange. Matt doesn't usually have bad luck. Not on the soccer pitch.

A few minutes later Matt does an overhead volley from a corner. The ball slams into the crossbar.

'Magic,' says Ayo.

'So unlucky,' moans Uncle Cliff.

Soon after, Matt shoots again. He hits the goalpost again.

All around the stadium people are turning to each other and there's a huge growling buzz. I realise it's the noise thousands of people make when they're not quite believing what they're seeing.

Matt does a long run with the ball, almost the full length of the pitch. Just gliding past tackles. He makes it look as easy as Dad avoiding chandeliers with a mirror.

The Chelsea goalie comes out to him. Matt skips past him and shoots at an empty goal.

And hits the post.

We all can't believe it.

'Arghhhhh,' screeches Uncle Cliff. 'Unbelievable bad luck.'

It happens again, from a diving header. And then again, from a clever lob near the touchline.

Ten minutes later, when Matt has hit the post three more times and the crossbar twice, people are just gaping as if they simply can't believe what's happening.

'This isn't just bad luck,' croaks Uncle Cliff. 'This is some sort of family curse.'

The players on both teams are glancing at each other nervously as if they're all having a similar thought. That something really spooky is going on. Which it is, but not in the way they're thinking.

Mrs Jarvis isn't saying anything, just watching Matt closely. I think she may have spotted what I think I've spotted.

Matt does it again, and this time I'm definitely sure. After blocking a pass thirty metres from the Chelsea goal, Matt gets his balance and shoots. But before he does, he glances at Jean-Pierre Michel, and then at Ayo.

The shot reaches the goal before the goalie can move. It smashes off the crossbar.

And that's when I know.

This isn't bad luck, or a family curse.

Matt is doing it on purpose.

42

At half-time the stadium is in uproar.

More than forty thousand people utterly gobsmacked and yelling about it into their phones.

Pandemonium.

Which is nothing compared to what's happening in Jean-Pierre Michel's office. I think there are about forty thousand people in here.

Matt is sitting on a chair in the corner, surrounded by people.

Me and Uncle Cliff and Mrs Jarvis and Ayo struggle over towards him through the crowd of journalists and media people and club officials.

'What you did was remarkable,' Jean-Pierre Michel is shouting at Matt over the hubbub. 'I've never seen anything like it. The accuracy and mental discipline to hit the post that many times, incredible. We want to offer you a permanent place in the academy.'

He waits to see if Matt has heard him.

'It wasn't just remarkable,' Uncle Cliff yells at Mr Michel. 'It was the most generous act ever seen on a sporting field ever. Including when the Rolling Stones did two encores at Randwick racecourse in 1973.'

'I agree,' I say.

I wasn't actually at Randwick racecourse back then, but I was here today and I'll never forget what Matt did, or why he did it.

Ever.

Jean-Pierre Michel glances at Uncle Cliff, but you can see he doesn't really want to talk about why Matt did it.

Matt isn't saying anything.

But when he sees Ayo, he gives him a look.

Ayo gives him a look back.

I can see Ayo won't ever forget what Matt did either.

'A full permanent place in the academy,' Jean-Pierre Michel is saying to Matt. 'We see you being in our first team regularly very soon.'

'Absolutely see you there,' says Mr Merchant. 'I'll put money on it.'

Matt is looking at them all now, but it's hard to tell what he's thinking.

'Matt's fourteen,' says Mrs Jarvis to Mr Michel. 'Full academy places are for boys of sixteen and over. There are regulations.'

'We know about the regulations,' says Ken.

'Matt will live with his family till he's sixteen. We'll bring his parents over and find them jobs and a house.'

I don't know about Matt, but I'm feeling a bit dazed by all this.

'What do you say, Matt?' says Jean-Pierre Michel.

I know what I'm hoping Matt will say.

And he says it.

'I want Ayo to play in the second half,' says Matt. 'With me.'

'Yes,' I say.

I don't expect anyone to hear me, but Mrs Jarvis puts her arm round me and I can see she heard. And she knows why I'm looking at Matt so proudly.

Jean-Pierre Michel frowns. You can tell he was half expecting Matt to say that. He looks at Ayo and at Mr Merchant.

'Ayo's a good young player,' says Mr Merchant. 'We only decided to let him go because of a problem with his manager. We can do this.'

'Good,' says Jean-Pierre Michel.

He turns back to Matt.

'So, young man,' he says. 'No need to hit any more woodwork, eh?'

It's nearly time for the second half. The officials steer Matt and Ayo through the crowd. But before they go out, Matt turns and looks at me.

He grins.

I grin back.

Suddenly I can breathe more easily than I have for years.

In fact I could do cartwheels down the pitch right now. Because now I know that whatever happens in the future, Matt will always be Matt, and his dear gentle loving heart will be alive and kicking forever.

43

What's happening in the second half of this Premier League match against Chelsea is one of the most joyful things I've ever seen on a soccer pitch, including our waste ground at home.

The reporters and commentators in the press boxes are going bananas. I can see them doing it through their tinted glass. It's like they never imagined they'd ever see anything like this.

But it's really quite simple.

Two fourteen-year-old boys are doing the thing they love best. Fast passing and good balance and very quick running and brilliant footwork and being happy and saying encouraging things to each other.

Matt sets the goals up and Ayo scores them.

Two in ten minutes.

I can see Jean-Pierre Michel and the other club officials down in their seats. They all look totally ecstatic. Every time Matt touches the ball they're on their feet, applauding. Same when Ayo does.

On the pitch the grown-up players are mesmerised.

Except suddenly they aren't. Now they're starting to realise that having kids running rings round them isn't very good for their careers.

Gradually the Chelsea players start to get back into the game. Lots of skill, and some of the other stuff. Holding and turning and a bit of violent lunging.

Mostly Matt and Ayo are too quick for them.

Our grown-up players don't want to be left out, so they start working extra hard too, turning on the skill and giving as good as they get.

A bit more than they get sometimes, and Chelsea end up with a free kick just outside our penalty area.

They score.

Two–two.

'Oh-oh,' mutters Uncle Cliff. 'Things could go pear-shaped now.'

'I don't think so, Cliff,' says Mrs Jarvis. 'We're playing a four-two-four formation. That's more peanut-shaped. Pear-shaped would be four-four-one-one.'

Uncle Cliff looks at her and just from his face you can tell he reckons he's the luckiest man in the world.

But he's right about the match. Things aren't going so well for us.

Chelsea score again, and then for about fifteen minutes their defence keeps Matt and Ayo locked down with very good tackles and not so good elbows.

But gradually Chelsea start to relax. You can see them thinking to themselves, these two are just kids.

Which is not a good idea with Matt.

He nips in and cuts off a Chelsea pass about thirty metres out from their goal and then there's one of those moments when forty-four thousand people blink and go dead silent for about two seconds and then thirty-four thousand of them give a humungous roar because the ball is in the back of the net.

I don't care that much about the goal.

What I care about is that as Matt shoots, just after the ball leaves his foot, he's crashed into by two Chelsea defenders. He slams into the pitch like a sack of pet food dropped by a careless removal man (not Dad).

I jump to my feet. Matt isn't moving. His tiny figure is lying down there, way below us on the pitch.

I have to get to him. But I'm high up in a vast stadium. Thousands of people are in the way. Hundreds of steps. Dozens of jammed walkways.

Mrs Jarvis puts her hand on my cheek.

'Go,' she says.

Uncle Cliff nods. He thinks I should too.

So I do.

'Matty,' I hear Uncle Cliff yelling. 'Bridie's coming.'

It takes me about five minutes of leaping down concrete steps and squeezing past rows of seats and ducking under crash barriers. But I'm still quicker than Uncle Cliff or Mrs Jarvis could be because people kindly lift me down from section to section over other people's heads.

At last I'm on the edge of the pitch.

I see Matt has been carried off and is sitting on a stretcher near the medical bench. A physio is rubbing his legs.

I rush over. I'm breathless and frantic and my heart's going like an Uncle Cliff drum solo, but the weird thing is, I'm not wheezing.

'Matt,' I say. 'Are you OK?'

Matt signals me to come closer. The physio steps back to give us some privacy, which is kind of him.

'I'm fine,' says Matt. 'I just thought Ayo should have a bit of time on his own to show the club why they should hang on to him.'

He points to the pitch.

I turn and look.

As I do, the stadium explodes with noise because Ayo blocks a pass, weaves past two defenders, does a step-over to confuse the goalie, glances at Matt, and scores.

Just before Ayo disappears under a pile of our players, he gives Matt a thumbs up.

Matt gives him one back.

Then stands up and gives me a hug.

'I'm not making a habit of all this cuddly stuff,' he says. 'It's just that last time we did some, you were pretty upset.'

I nod.

'And it was my fault,' he says.

I don't say anything.

Matt doesn't either for a while. When I look up at him, I see his eyes are wet.

I think that's amazing. There aren't many big brothers who'd show their feelings in front of forty-four thousand people.

'Are you OK?' I say.

'Very OK now,' he says. 'Thanks to you.'

We keep our arms round each other for a couple more minutes till the match is over.

But not completely over, because there's some embarrassing stuff that always happens afterwards when a side has just beaten a really huge club like Chelsea.

It's sort of like extra time, but it's not more football. It's a lap of honour round the stadium by the winning team so their fans can yell themselves silly with joy.

The most embarrassing thing is when certain players get carried on the shoulders of the rest of the team.

Like what's happening now to Matt and Ayo.

And me.

I know I'm not a player, but they insisted.

'Who are you again?' asks the legendary Spanish international who's carrying me on his shoulders.

Matt grins and reaches over and pulls some of the paper streamers off my head.

'This is Bridie,' he says. 'We're family.'

I give him a huge grin back.

That's exactly Judas H right.

Thanks from the author

My heartfelt gratitude to Belinda Chayko,
Anna Fienberg, Laura Harris, Heather Curdie,
Tony Palmer, Anne McNulty, Amrit Bansal-McNulty,
Janine Wood, Sam Miller, and the Premier League
families who generously shared with me their
experiences and friendship.

About the author

Morris Gleitzman grew up in England and moved to
Australia when he was sixteen. After university he
worked for ten years as a screenwriter. Then he had
a wonderful experience. He wrote a novel for young
people. Now, after thirty-four books, he's one of
Australia's most popular children's authors. His books
are published in more than twenty countries.

Visit Morris at his website:
www.morrisgleitzman.com

More books to enjoy
by Morris Gleitzman

Bumface

His mum calls him Mr Dependable,
but Angus can barely cope. Another baby would
be a disaster. So Angus comes up with a bold and
brave plan to stop her getting pregnant.
That's when he meets Rindi.
And Angus thought *he* had problems . . .

Two Weeks With The Queen

'I need to see the Queen about my sick brother.'

Colin Mudford is on a quest. His brother is very ill and
the doctors in Australia don't seem to be able to cure
him. Colin reckons it's up to him to find the best doctor
in the world. And how better to do this than by asking
the Queen for help?

'A moving and page-turning book' – Sunday Times

Boy Overboard

Jamal and Bibi have a dream. To lead Australia
to soccer glory in the next World Cup.
But first they must face landmines,
pirates, storms and assassins.
Can Jamal and his family survive their
incredible journey and get to Australia?

MORRIS GLEITZMAN

Everybody
deserves
to have
something good in their life.

At least
Once.

Once

Once I escaped from an orphanage
to find Mum and Dad.
Once I saved a girl called Zelda from a burning house.
Once I made a Nazi with a toothache laugh.
My name is Felix.
This is my story.

Then

I had a plan for me and Zelda.
Pretend to be someone else.
Find new parents.
Be safe forever.
Then the Nazis came.

After

After the Nazis took my parents I was scared.

After they killed my best friend I was angry.

After they ruined my thirteenth birthday I was determined.

To get to the forest.

To join forces with Gabriek and Yuli.

To be a family.

To defeat the Nazis after all.

Now

Once I didn't know about my grandfather Felix's
scary childhood. Then I found out what the Nazis
did to his best friend Zelda. Now I understand
why Felix does the things he does.
At least he's got me.
My name is Zelda too.
This is our story.